The Banker and the Empath

The Banker Trilogy, Volume 3

Martin Lundqvist

Published by Martin Lundqvist, 2021.

THE BANKER AND THE EMPATH

First edition. January 17, 2021.

Written by Martin Lundqvist.

Chapter 1: Pierre Beaumont sets up a competition to find a suitable heir. 23rd October 2039.

Pierre Beaumont was holding the Zetan Monocle belonging to the fallen Ben Yehuda in his right hand. It felt poignant to him that one of the members of the Monocle Conspiracy had fallen, but Pierre had done what he could to bring Ben back to life. Pierre thought back on how Ben had died on that day, almost two years earlier.

Ben had reported that they had found Keila Eisenstein, who they believed to be the only one able to open the gate at Solomon Temple that blocked the entrance to where primordial Zeto Crystal was located. Keila Eisenstein was a fake persona, the real identity of the mysterious girl was the 18-year-old Sabina Hines, a lone traveller from Australia. The fact she had chosen the alias Keila Eisenstein had to mean something. Ben Yehuda and Martin Orchard had come up with a plan to lure Sabina Hines to the Templar Tunnels at Solomon Temple, so she could open the locked ancient gate. The plan had worked, and Sabina had managed to open the gate. Straight after that, things had turned bad. Martin Orchard had turned against his comrade Ben Yehuda and his fellow Templars and murdered them all. Martin had helped Sabina escape with the Zeto crystal and he had closed the gate, leaving the dead bodies of Ben and the Templars inside the temple. Mossad agents, led by Ben's brother Szymon Yehuda, had tracked Martin down and killed him, but the Zeto Crystal and Sabina Hines were nowhere to be found.

In the current time, Pierre was studying the lifeless body of Martin Orchard, which was frozen in a cryogenic tank. If Pierre chose to, he could resurrect Martin and punish him for his betrayal. Instead, he chose to let Martin remain dead in a permanent slumber. With Ben Yehuda, things were different. Upon Martin's betrayal, Vladimir and Szymon had been tasked to find a replicated Zeto Crystal to once again open the gate. Yet, as finding a replicated Zeto Crystal took time, they had come too late and Ben Yehuda's corpse had already decomposed when they got to him. Ben had been beyond resurrection, even with the powers of a replicated Zeto Crystal. However, a primordial Zeto Crystal could potentially still revive him. While Pierre had suggested that they would freeze Ben Yehuda's remains until they had the primordial Zeto Crystal, Szymon had been against it. They were too late, and Szymon felt compelled to continue his Jewish Supremacy plan on his own. They had cremated Ben Yehuda, and Pierre had kept Ben's Zetan Monocle for himself.

Pierre read the intelligence file on Sabina Hines. Sabina was now 20 years old, living in Sydney, running a charity to protect the environment. She had used the power of the primordial Zeto Crystal to make a fortune from trading the financial markets under a variety of fake aliases. Officially, Sabina Hines and her husband Alexander O'Neill were the directors of the environment-focused "Building a Better World" charity. Knowing that she owned the primordial crystal, Pierre suspected that she had other hidden motivations.

At first, Pierre had planned to send Vladimir to Australia to murder Sabina in secrecy. But then he had feared that all the other Zetan Monocle conspiracists that were also searching for the crystal would kill him if he attained it, and so he decided to let her go, for now. Having followed Sabina's actions for the last few years, he had foreseen that she was more gifted than any of his children. It would be ideal if she were to join the Monocle Conspiracy and serve him.

Pierre shook off the idea. Everything indicated that Sabina was a bleeding-heart do-gooder, and she was unlikely to serve him. To achieve his goals, he needed to get his own children more involved in his prime mission. The 24 children he had from the surrogacy breeding projects had turned 16, so they were ready to serve him and it was now time to choose a suitable heir.

Pierre creeped down to his old and musty-smelling wine cellar to fetch a bottle of vintage wine. His knee joints were creaking, and he realised that old age was catching up with him. He was 70 years old, and his body was in a bad shape from his stressful lifestyle and heavy drinking. *I should have ordered the servants to fetch the bottle for me,'* Pierre thought, and brushed the thought off.

He couldn't allow himself to be seen as weak to his obedient servants. How could he rule the world if he couldn't even fetch his own drink?

Pierre picked up a bottle of red vintage wine, dragged himself up the stairs, and poured a glass of wine in front of the warm and cosy fireplace. He turned on his hologram laptop, and organised an exciting competition among his 24 children, to find a suitable heir.

A 16-YEAR-OLD BRUNETTE girl, Delphine Beaumont, studied her reflection in the full-body mirror in her room, in Pierre's Swiss Alps heritage centre. *'This is where we will shape the future of House Beaumont and the fate of the world.'* Delphine mumbled. She sighed, hesitated, and shook off the thought. How could she be a future world leader, if she had lived the first 16 years of her life as a prisoner to her distant, cold, and awful father?

"Urrgh!" Delphine exclaimed as she picked up a glass and threw it at the mirror, shattering it into thousands of small fragments. She hated watching her reflection. It reminded her of her father, and in her eyes, she was as ugly as him. She remembered what Pierre had told her during one of their formal meetings in the last year. "I chose your mother as the IVF donor because she was my cousin, in order to preserve Beaumont heritage. Beauty is on the outside and it fades. You should feel proud that you have a true Beaumont bloodline."

Delphine hated her father. Pierre had spoken about herself and her mother, whom she had never met, as if they were racehorses that he bred genetically to serve a purpose to fulfil his wishes. Here she was, a 16-year-old girl produced genetically by artificial insemination, born through a surrogate mother, who never laid eyes upon her, and her purpose was everything she knew in her life. As much as she hated Pierre, her main purpose was to win the competition and become Pierre's ultimate heir, what else was there to live for?

The supervisor of the breeding facility, Constance Monet rushed into Delphine's room, looked at the shattered mirror, and reproached her:

- What is the meaning of this, Delphine?

Delphine:

- I hate this ugly mirror. I hate the way I look! I hate the way it reminds me of him.

Constance shook Delphine and spoke:

- Be quiet, spoiled child. You're living in a facility that prepares you for leading the world in the Beaumont legacy. Strength comes from determination and the willingness to succeed. It doesn't come from self-loathing and hatred.

Delphine clenched her jaw and looked at shards of the broken mirror. She wanted to slit the throat of her superintendent Constance, to get her revenge for all the torture and scorn she had experienced all these years. Constance spoke again:

- I know you want to attack me, Delphine. But it wouldn't serve you. If you kill me, my guards will kill you, and you'll lose your shot at the power you're so close to obtaining.

Delphine took a deep breath and swallowed her anger. Constance spoke again:

- Good. With that out of the way, please come with me. Mr Beaumont has summoned all his offspring to meet him at the grand dining room.

Delphine sighed and walked towards the door. Before she got out, Constance scorned her:

- Do you want to meet your father dressed like that? Dress appropriately. You are not a child anymore, silly girl!

Without another word, Delphine walked to her walk-in wardrobe, put on the Beaumont Family school uniform, and walked towards the dining room.

PIERRE FELT PROUD OF himself as he entered The Beaumont Family Heritage centre, where his loyal superintendent operatives raised his children. The construction of the centre took place in 2022, and it contained all the modern technologies, particularly surveillance technologies. Pierre's crew had built the centre in resemblance to the old boarding school he had attended when he was a child, before the Beaumont family's fall from grace. Visiting the centre, Pierre remembered his happy childhood years. Things were so different before the tragic accident that killed his parents and sister, and the suicide of his grandpa that followed.

Pierre looked at his children, who had lined up in unison at the dining hall. The tables were set in a U-shape. The facility supervisors sat at the centre of the table, all the boys were sitting at the right-hand-side and all the girls were sitting on the left-hand-side. The children were all facing the centre of the room and podium. It was a beautiful symmetry, which would be lost when he chose one child to stay with him. Such was the plight of life; perfect symmetry could not last forever.

Pierre walked up to the stand on the podium and spoke:

- Greetings, children.

- Today is a great day, because one of you will receive the privilege of leaving this facility and come to live with me at Palace Beaumont.

- I have put together a series of tests to determine who is the most suitable to become my successor. Do your best, but don't be distraught if you are not selected. The world is large enough for all of you to dominate it, together as a Beaumont family.

- I'll leave it to your superintendents to carry out the testing.

- However, I urge you to remember. Big Father is always watching.

Having said this, Pierre left the dining hall and walked towards the surveillance room where all the CCTV footage was available for him to see. This was his preferred way of interacting with his progeny, always watching from afar and giving them instructions via the speakers.

THE FOLLOWING DAY, Pierre was reviewing the competition results from the previous night's trials and tribulations. He smiled when he saw how Delphine had aced all her tests, closely followed by her twin brother, Lucien. The stupid and deformed Raphael had failed all tests, as usual. It was as if he intentionally failed on everything to gain Pierre's attention, which Pierre found bothersome. The emotive screening cameras didn't indicate that Raphael felt depressed, in fact he was happy that he failed. Genetic testing on Raphael hadn't found the cause for his deformity, lack of ambition and perceived unintelligence.

Pierre smiled when he anticipated the shock it would cause to his children when he announced that Raphael would be his winning selection. How they reacted to this announcement was the intention of the whole testing procedure. In actuality, the son or daughter who could rise to the occasion, the first runner-up to Raphael, was to be the one he would select as his real heir. Pierre had felt ashamed when he had been sidestepped in favour of the fat bastard Gunter Fritz while they were both working at the Deutsche Bank in Germany. Since then, he had come out stronger from the ordeal, and it was his burning desire for revenge to make Beaumont family the ultimate world leaders, that had made him the wealthiest and most powerful man in the world.

Having made up his mind, Pierre entered the auditorium to disclose his shocking decision.

PIERRE WAS WALKING to his car, accompanied by Constance Monet and Raphael Beaumont, when Delphine ran after them. She shouted:

- Pierre! Hold on. I need to talk to you.

Constance leaned in and whispered in Pierre's ear:

- Be careful, Monsieur Beaumont. Delphine is volatile and she was close to attacking me yesterday with a shard of broken glass.

Pierre smirked and replied:

- Thank you, Constance. But I have nothing to fear from the sweet and innocent Delphine. I am sure a few words will alleviate her worries.

Pierre turned to Delphine and spoke:

- Refer to me as Big Father or Father Beaumont. Addressing one's father by the first name is disrespectful.

Delphine:

- I don't care. How could you pick Raphael over me? I aced all the tests, while he failed everything!

Pierre:

- You are correct, Delphine. You did ace all the tests. However, I never said that acing the tests was the desirable outcome. That was something you incorrectly assumed.

Delphine held back her tears. She felt distraught knowing how unfair Pierre was to her. Knowing that she was not the winner, she would never get out of the horrible and cold breeding facility centre. How could it have come to this? She fitted all the criteria of an excellent daughter, and he had told her that she was his favourite daughter on one occasion. Pierre walked up to Delphine and touched her face, a spitting image of himself. Delphine sniffed and said:

- I hate you! How can you do this to me?

Pierre:

- You'll understand in due time. Besides, succeeding me is not your true desire. Do what you truly desire, and you'll be free.

Hearing this, Delphine let out her tears. Pierre took his old and frail hand away from her unappealing face, took a few steps back, and spoke again:

> - Unfortunately, our time is up for today, Delphine. I need to focus on Raphael now. But we will meet again. Take care, and keep your faith in me.

Having said this, Pierre and Raphael entered his private limousine, which took them back to Palace Beaumont.

Chapter 2: "Raphael is the worst part of me." 30th October 2039

Pierre Beaumont wrinkled in disgust, as he watched the CCTV footage of his mentally disabled son Raphael, sitting in his room by himself. Raphael had taken some lint from his own navel, tasted it, spat it out and looked at the camera with a silly grimace. Pierre turned off the computer. Observing Raphael's lack of intelligence would not bring more ideas to his evil mission. Pierre concluded that he had to interact with Raphael. "Mon Dieu, Raphael is the worst part of me," Pierre muttered to himself as he walked towards Raphael's room, on the top-level of the luxurious mansion.

Pierre walked towards the stairs, but his knees tormented him as he ascended the staircase in agony. He needed double knee surgery, and a long period of rehab to get them better, but he didn't have time for such pursuits. Age was catching up with him and he needed to achieve a lot more to secure his lineage. The Beaumonts were meant to rule the world, and it was Pierre's obligation to make it happen.

Pierre's assistant, Jean Valmont, approached him and spoke:

- Monsieur Beaumont! I am worried about your knees. Let me fetch Raphael for you.

Pierre gave Jean a sceptical look, and replied with a condescending tone:

- Hrmph! Don't worry about my knees. They are merely dysfunctional pieces of bone, ligament and muscle. The only thing that matters, my brain, is still in peak performance. As for fetching Raphael,

I do not intend to let my knees stopping me from walking around in my own palace!

Jean:

- Apologies, sir. I didn't mean to offend you.

Pierre sighed:

- It's okay, Jean. You have worked for me for 18 years and you still haven't learnt how to respect me. I find small doses of your disrespect strangely refreshing. But don't go overboard, yes?

Jean:

- Alright, master. Perhaps we can install an elevator in here? That way you can move around in the palace without pain.

Pierre:

- Hrmph! The Beaumont family has inhabited this palace for centuries. Do you see any lift? My forebears could walk in these stairs, and so will I. Dismissed, Jean.

Hearing this, Jean bowed and rushed off. Pierre smiled as she went out of sight. Jean had been working for almost two decades and she was a fixture in his life. A source of annoyance for sure, but still a point of reference.

As Jean was often seen near Pierre, the tabloids were speculating that they were a couple. Pierre didn't mind, as a matter of fact, he encouraged it. If the media spent time speculating about his sex life, that meant they wouldn't investigate on more perilous parts of his life, such as how he had contaminated New York City's water supply with the Hei Bai virus; or how his drug manufacturing company had released a medication that killed the virus but also caused a lot of dangerous side effects; or how he meddled in governmental elections.

Pierre's phone rang. The display showed 'Danielle Anders, Australian Prime Minister'. Pierre ignored the call and kept walking towards Raphael's room. His puppet Prime Minister of Australia could wait a while.

RAPHAEL WAS LYING IN bed while watching a broadcasted video on his tablet. He was swooning over a press conference with the young, famous, and beautiful environmentalist Sabina Hines. The press conference described how robotic sea drones would clean up the Pacific Ocean. Raphael had never been to the ocean, but it looked beautiful and he hoped he could meet with Sabina.

Pierre entered the room and Raphael grinned and turned off the tablet. Pierre taunted:

- Are you watching porn, Raphael?

Raphael giggled and replied:

- No. Of course not.

Pierre:

- Very well. Then show me what you're watching.

Raphael turned on the tablet, showed the video to Pierre, and said:

- Isn't this amazing. She is so young and has such big dreams. I wish our tutors told us about her.

Pierre hid his disapproval. He had confined his progeny to a secret location and asked his superintendents to shape the children in his image. He had also programmed the AI to block all mentions of persons and events that didn't fit Pierre's future vision. As it would seem, nothing of this had worked as his son had become a teenage fanboy of the virtue-signalling Sabina Hines.

Pierre:

- Sabina is all talk. What has she ever done for the world?

- Your Father, on the other hand, saved humanity from doom when the evil Hei Bai virus ravaged our planet in 2021. We dispersed medication that helped the world.

Raphael:

- But I don't understand, Father. If you are such a benevolent man, why are your children confined to the boarding school in the Beaumont Heritage Centre? Why do you never show us any love?

Pierre:

- Don't engage in self-pity, Raphael. Sealing you off from the world was my gift to you. You grew up in a safe environment, where you received first-class care, nutrition, and education. That is more than most humans receive.

Raphael:

- I am in love with Sabina Hines. Can't we go see her, Father? I would love to travel to Australia to visit her. We can make Sabina's vision come true with our family's wealth.

Pierre thought of slapping Raphael, but he controlled himself. There was not a chance in hell that he would introduce his son to the fraud Sabina, who had stolen the primordial Zeto Crystal from him. Pierre:

- Hmmph. I just received an important financial news update via my monocle. I'll need to address this issue immediately. I'll speak to you later, Raphael.

Having said this, Pierre turned around, and strode towards the door, ignoring the agonising pain in his knees.

DELPHINE BEAUMONT WAS crying herself to sleep. She was furious with Pierre. He had dared to tell her to follow her dreams, while on the other hand keeping her as a prisoner at this boarding school / breeding facility. What had the old bastard meant by following her dreams? Delphine hated everyone, especially her indifferent siblings, and she wanted it all to end.

Delphine wiped away her tears and she forced a smile. There was one person she didn't hate in this facility. In fact, she adored him. It was her twin brother, Lucien Beaumont. When she was around him, she felt a tingling emotion and he had filled her with exciting wet dreams. Delphine held back. Was she in love with her brother, or was it the lack of other romantic options that caused him to be the focal point of her carnal desire?

Delphine opened a book about the pyramids and the ancient Egyptians. The Egyptians had always impressed Delphine. She loved their ability to build structures that could withstand the tests of time. Another thing fascinated her. The Pharaohs had married their sibling to keep the bloodline pure from the lower classes. Was this the reason she was locked up in this facility, together with her siblings?

Delphine studied herself in the mirror. Why had they put a new mirror in her room, a few days after she destroyed the other one? It didn't make any sense, yet she couldn't stay away from her reflection. Delphine stared in a mix of terror and fascination, as her reflection slowly turned to that of a hideous monstrosity. The monstrosity in front of her was no longer a shy 16-year-old little girl, it was now a humanoid creature with ugly fangs and purple predatoric eyes. The creature hissed:

- Delphine Beaumont, we meet at last. I have been observing you from a distance. Growl!

Delphine:

- Who are you?

Ugly Creature:

- I am Empress Rangda Kaliankan, and you have a rare gene that allows us to communicate to each other.

Delphine:

- What gene are you talking about?

Empress Rangda:

- Silence! Our connection is weak and our time is short. You need to fulfil your destiny. You need to breed with Lucien, kill your father, and then take his place. You'll create a dynasty that will rule humankind....!

Delphine:

- But how would I do any of this?

Empress Rangda:

- Your brother will accept your sexual advances. Seduce him, and murder the guard who will fall asleep in the guardhouse next Monday. Steal the guard's weapons, set the building on fire, and murder everyone as they try to escape.

Delphine:

- Who are you, and why are you telling me this?!

Delphine didn't receive any response. Instead, her reflection quickly reverted back to her usual self, and the voice was now gone. Delphine screamed and collapsed to the floor in shock. A few minutes later, the facility guards entered her room, gave her sedatives to silence her erratic behaviour, and put her to sleep in her bed.

'I CANNOT LISTEN TO Raphael talking about Sabina Hines any longer!!' Pierre muttered as he left Raphael's room in frustration. His son had petitioned that they should travel together to Sydney, Australia and meet with Sabina.

Pierre had pretended to agree, since it was crucial to gain Raphael's complete trust for the next part of his malicious plan.

Pierre walked to his office, unlocked a biometric safe, and took out the deceased Ben Yehuda's Zetan monocle. It was time to give the Zetan gadget to Raphael, to silence his idiotic tendencies.

Pierre had postponed the testing of the monocle on Raphael's small head. If he failed to deactivate the monocle's automatic defences, it would identify Raphael as an unauthorised user and kill him. Pierre had thought of sparing Raphael's life by not making him wear it. However, having listened to Raphael's foolish ideologies for almost a week, Pierre had concluded that he would be the first candidate for the monocle, and thus the perfect test subject.

Pierre picked up the monocle and walked to Raphael's room. Raphael gave him a confused look when he entered the room again. Raphael said:

- Father, why are you back so soon? I thought you would make the arrangements for our trip to Sydney.

'Spoiled brat. Treating his father as a servant to fulfil his whims and wishes,' Pierre thought and replied:

- Before I can organise a meeting with Sabina Hines, Raphael darling, I need you to put this on. It contains an advanced AI that helped me become the wealthiest man in the world.

Raphael received the Zetan Monocle and he studied it carefully. It didn't look particularly impressive, although it looked like the one his Father wore, but Raphael sensed a mystical aura emitting from the monocle. 'Don't put it on.' He heard a faint female voice whisper. He turned to Pierre and spoke:

- Hold on. How did you get your hands on this monocle before you were wealthy? How is that possible? I thought your scientists made these for you?

'He is a lot more alert than meets the eye,' Pierre thought and replied:

- When I got the monocle, our family was already wealthy and powerful, but the AI of this monocle made me the wealthiest man on the planet.

Raphael was excited with Pierre's answer and he replied:

- So, when was it made, who made it for you, and what are the technical specifications?

'No point in lying to the boy, who has the potential to be my heir if he is able to activate it,' Pierre thought and replied:

- I found it during an expedition in Nepal. We were a group of nine individuals that came across an ancient alien temple belonging to the Zetan race. One person from our group died a few years ago, and I am passing on his monocle to you.

Raphael shook his head and gave Pierre a funny look. Raphael said:

- Stop mocking me, dad. If you don't want to tell me where you got it, that's ok. But do you promise that we'll meet with Sabina Hines if I try on this gadget?

'If you survive.' Pierre thought and replied:

- Yes, we will. If you follow my directions, we'll go to Australia and meet that idol of yours. With a bit of luck, you'll realise that she is just a seller of pipe dreams and nothing else.

Raphael agreed and looked at the monocle again. *'It's a trap, you'll die, Raphael!'* The faint female voice whispered again. Raphael turned to Pierre and spoke:

- Is there someone else in the room? Is this one of your tests?

Pierre:

- Look, I don't have all day. If you don't follow my instructions, I won't organise the meeting with Sabina Hines.

Hearing this, Raphael inserted the monocle and Pierre sensed how his mind connected to Raphael. *'Unauthorised user connected to Monocle 005, preparing to terminate the user.'* popped up on Pierre's display. *'Monocle 001 demands to override usage restriction on Monocle 005.'* Pierre sent back. *'Usage changing request denied. A consensus is required to change user settings.'* Raphael's monocle replied.

Pierre's perception of time slowed to a standstill. A timer was counting down in slow motion. If he couldn't get the other members of the Monocle Conspiracy to approve Raphael as the Monocle's new owner, his son would die. *'I need to contact everyone at once'* Pierre thought, but he stopped himself. He would need Martin Orchard's approval to unlock the Zetan Monocle and that couldn't happen as Martin was frozen inside a cryogenic tank.

Time resumed and Pierre exclaimed:

- Raphael. You need to take off the monocle!

Raphael:

- Why, Father?

Time slowed down for Pierre. *'4 seconds to termination of the unauthorised user.'* Pierre's monocle showed. *"Mon Dieu, I don't have the time for this!"* Pierre thought. He would have to pull Raphael's monocle out of his small head, leaving him blind on one eye, but he would still live.

Time resumed and Pierre jumped towards Raphael and tried to grab the Zetan monocle. The attempt was unsuccessful, as the monocle's forcefield electrocuted Pierre, and sent him flying backwards into the wall. Pierre looked in horror on the severe burns on his hand.

There was a shriek of pain and agony, and Raphael collapsed next to Pierre. The monocle had disfigured Raphael's face and blood poured out from his right eye.

Chapter 3: "It runs in the family", 1ˢᵗ November 2039

Pierre felt a little distraught as he studied the lifeless body of his son Raphael, who was now lying in a puddle of blood in one of the Palace Beaumont guestrooms. The first rays of the morning sun were entering through a window and Pierre had been sitting like this since the disastrous accident the previous night.

Pierre had planned to use Raphael to unlock the ownership, and then reprogram the monocle to a new user. This was the reason he had tested the Zetan Monocle on Raphael instead of his preferred successor, Delphine. Pierre had brushed off his concerns and he had felt convinced that he could disable the safeguards while also not killing Raphael. Not until the last seconds had he realised the terrifying truth. To disable the monocles safeguard, he needed permission from all other monocle users. With Martin Orchard dead in a cryogenic tank, this had failed miserably, and he had failed to transfer the monocle's ownership from the deceased Ben Yehuda.

Pierre knew what he needed to do. In order to give Ben Yehuda's monocle to Delphine and make her his true heir, he needed to revive Martin Orchard and make him agree to the transfer. This was the only way to achieve his goals.

Pierre's trusted assassin and occasional gay lover, Vladimir Kravchenko, entered the room. He walked up to Pierre and spoke:

- I have turned off our security cameras and sent our employees home. Let's get Raphael's body to the cryogenic tanks.

Pierre shook his head and replied:

- Take Raphael's body to the furnace. I don't want to revive him.

Vladimir gave Pierre a quick look and replied:

- Why? After complaining all night about how you lost your son, I thought we would drag ourselves across the world to find a Zeto Crystal and revive him.

Pierre:

- I will send you on a quest to find a Zeto Crystal, but we are reviving someone else. We are reviving Martin Orchard.

Vladimir:

- Why are you sacrificing your son's life to save that traitor? What is going on in that genius brain of yours? Tsk, tsk, tsk.

Pierre:

- I have to revive Martin Orchard to deactivate the monocle defences that stop me from giving Ben's monocle to Delphine, my true heir.

- Besides, I am doing Raphael a favour. The peace of eternal death is preferable to the terrible toll of survival in this cruel world.

Vladimir:

- Yet, you brought me back from the dead in 2029?

Pierre smirked:

- You are a murderous monster, Vladimir. You deserve to suffer after your countless crimes against humanity, so I'm letting you live longer.

Vladimir burst into laughter and replied:

- Ha-ha, thanks Pierre. Now get your needed sleep. I will cover up Raphael's death on your behalf. When you wake up, it will be like he never even existed!

Pierre nodded, left the room, and returned to his bedroom. Before he fell asleep, he thought. *'I wish it was that easy. I wish I could convince myself that Raphael never existed. He was truly the worst part in me.'*

DELPHINE BEAUMONT STARED into her bedroom mirror. She wished to see the purple-eyed monster she had sighted the other night. She needed more guidance from this strange creature. The creature had told her to do the thing she desired more than anything in life. It had told her to fuck her twin brother, and kill the rest of her father's progeny so she could rule House Beaumont together with Lucien. But it was all too convenient to have this vision now, and she could not be sure that it wasn't a mental illness that gave her hallucinations. If she went through with her advances, the most likely scenario was that Lucien would reject her sexual advances. Even if he embraced her advances, it would still be difficult and dangerous to kill the guards and the rest of her siblings at this facility.

'It doesn't matter. I rather die than live like this!' Delphine thought and she prepared herself for her plan. The door to her room was locked, but she had petitioned Constance Monet to leave her window unlocked, stating her need for fresh mountain air to stay healthy. *'They must not consider me suicidal, or they don't care if I die.'* Delphine thought as she opened the windows and stared into the dark abyss.

The Beaumont Family heritage centre was built on top of a mountain and Delphine's room faced a scenery to the valley below. If she lost her balance while sneaking from outside her windows to Lucien's room, she would plunge to her death.

Delphine shivered from the icy mountain wind that chilled her to the bone, as she was scantily clad in a thin nightgown. *'I don't want to die.'* She whimpered.

Delphine pushed aside her fears. Her entire life had come to this, and her father had told her to pursue what she desired. This was it. Delphine climbed out of the window and stood on the narrow path that led to her only source of happiness. On her right-hand side, there was death, but on her left-hand-side, 50 metres ahead of her, was her salvation in the form of Lucien's chiselled body.

'*Focus on your desires,*' Delphine thought as she pushed through her fear of death and soldiered on. In no time, she stood outside Lucien's room. Delphine looked through the window. Her twin brother was watching sensual videos, and was masturbating. '*Rangda was right, this was the right time to make a move.*'

Delphine knocked on the window and her brother stared at her in shock, awkwardly covering his erect penis. He opened the window and exclaimed:

 - What are you doing here, Delphine?!

Delphine smiled sweetly and replied:

 - Are you going to let me in, dear brother, or would you rather let me
   fall to my death?

Hearing this, Lucien hurried to pulled Delphine over the window ledge.

Once inside Lucien's room, Delphine didn't waste any time. She dropped her nightgown to the floor, pushed Lucien to his bed, got on top of him, and rode him furiously until they came.

PIERRE BEAUMONT WOKE up as his secretary Jean Valmont called him on the intercom. "Bloody woman, can't she book an appointment before calling me like everyone else?" Pierre muttered and looked at the wall clock in the corner of the room. It was midday, and he had slept for over sixteen hours.

Pierre recalled blurry images from the day before. Mourning the loss of his son, Pierre had agreed to the drugs Vladimir provided and submitted to his carnal desires. The night had been rough, very rough, but it had been necessary to embrace the pain to get closure and move on. Pierre limped to the full-size mirror and studied his shrivelled old body. There were wounds and bruises all over his wrinkly torso, courtesy of Vladimir's sadistic whip and sadomasochism from the night before. "Fucking hell. That was truly a great night. Vladimir's malicious whip will be the death of me." Pierre muttered to himself while licking his lips quietly.

"Mon Dieu. Monsieur Beaumont, what happened to you?"

Pierre turned around, gave his assistant Jean Valmont a stern look, and exclaimed:

- Why are you sneaking into my room, Jean?

Jean:

- I needed to check in on you, Master. You are not answering the intercom. I have been calling for 30 minutes non-stop.

Pierre:

- Next time, don't come in without my approval.
- But since you are here, why do you need to speak to me?

Jean:

- Constance Monet is here and she refuses to leave.

Pierre:

- Bah! Bloody woman. Tell her I'll meet with her soon.

Jean:

- Understood.
- Umm. Mr Beaumont. May I humbly ask, what happened to your body?

Pierre:

- That's none of your business! But if you have to know, book an appointment with Vladimir. I am sure he'll be happy to show you.

Hearing this, Jean nodded and rushed off. "Bloody woman," Pierre muttered. Of all the pains he had to deal with, his secretary was his biggest headache. Pierre shook his head, got dressed, and headed to the lounge room to deal with the next headache of the day, Constance Monet.

PIERRE FELT REFRESHED after doing a few lines of cocaine, before meeting with Constance. While drugs weren't the answer to his problems, they at least alleviated his migraine. As Pierre entered the lounge room, Constance Monet approached him and yelped:

- Master Pierre Beaumont! There has been a terrible development at the school!

Pierre gave Constance Monet a cold gaze and replied:

- Grummph. What's so terrible you can't book an appointment like my other employees?

Constance Monet handed Pierre a phone with the CCTV footage from Lucien's room, showcasing the incestual scene from the night before. Pierre looked at the video and struggled to hide his evil smile. Delphine had proven herself to be exactly what he wanted in his heir. She was a highly motivated risk-taker with her eyes fixated on the goal, willing to take any steps necessary to achieve it. This was her way of preserving the Beaumont bloodline, yet still satisfying her sexual needs. Pierre closed the video and turned to Constance:

- It runs in the family, Constance. I do not see this as a problem.

Constance:

- What do you mean?

Pierre:

- Never mind.
- Does anyone else know about this video?

Constance:

- No. I am the only one who has access to the videos from the student bedrooms.

Pierre:

- How convenient, I am sure you have a perfectly reasonable explanation for collecting secret videos from my children's bedrooms!

- In any case, if you don't like the copulation to take place, you should lock the windows to prevent further incidents.

Constance:

- But, Monsieur Beaumont. We need to deal with the issue straight away.

Pierre:

- Oh. Is that so? Alright, I'll just pop into my time machine, travel back to last night, and put a lock on Delphine's window.

- Oh, I don't have a time machine you say? Very well, then we'll have to live with what happened.

- Dismissed, Constance.

Having said this, Pierre turned around and left the room, ignoring Constance Monet's pleas for him to listen to her.

PIERRE WAS DRINKING red wine in a luxurious giraffe-leather armchair in front of the fireplace at the reading room of Palace Beaumont. He felt sleepy and exhausted. There were so many things that had happened in the last few days, and the drugs didn't make things better. Vladimir entered the room and spoke:

- I am afraid you'll need to find a new supervisor for your heritage centre.

Pierre:

- I wouldn't worry about that. Constance Monet is loyal and suitable for running the centre.

Vladimir:

- Constance Monet is dead. She died half an hour ago in a traffic accident. The AI in her self-driving car drove her off a cliff.

Pierre:

- What did you do, Vladimir? Did you kill her?

Vladimir:

- She was a threat to us, Pierre. She could have exposed what was going on at that place.

Pierre got up, slapped Vladimir, and spoke:

- You cannot kill my employees without my permission, Vladimir. I am their master; their lives are mine to decide.

Having reprimanded Vladimir, Pierre's perception of time froze. This could be it. Would he finally die by the hand of his lover, the Siberian gay sadist Vladimir Kravchenko? For what felt like an eternity, Vladimir stood silent and stared at Pierre. Eventually, he turned around and walked towards the door. "I'll be back to give you more punishments for your erratic behaviour." Vladimir stated as he left Palace Beaumont.

Chapter 4: Death and destruction at the Beaumont Heritage Centre. 6th November 2039.

Pierre Beaumont was enjoying the sunshine and the icy mountain winds at his terrace, wearing a bright-coloured skiing outfit. While his physique didn't allow him to do mountain skiing anymore, he still loved the refreshing feeling from inhaling the freezing air, and looking as fashionable as ever. Pierre looked at a photograph of his long-dead older sister Anna Beaumont. Anna had been beautiful, but at the time of her death, Pierre had been prepubescent, and he hadn't realised it. Once he reached puberty, he had become obsessed with Anna, and he couldn't make himself love another woman. Thus, instead of love, he had pursued wealth and the raw physical attraction he felt towards men.

Pierre picked up another photograph, the photo of his cousin, Luisa Beaumont, the unwilling biological mother of all his children. When Pierre had decided to run his breeding program, Anna had been dead and buried for over 40 years, and his younger cousin Luisa had been the closest Pierre could get to preserving the Beaumont heritage and bloodline. Luisa had not been interested in helping Pierre with his twisted scheme, but Vladimir had been. Together with Vladimir, they had kidnapped Luisa and kept her captive for six months while injecting her with drugs to make her constantly ovulate. Once they had made Luisa provide enough of her eggs, they had killed her to get rid of the evidence. They had used her eggs to then start a surrogacy foundation breeding program, using all of her collected eggs and Pierre's sperm to produce 24 children, forcing slaves to become the surrogate mothers.

Pierre sniffed arrogantly, thinking of Luisa's fate. Things had been so much better for her if she had agreed to help him. The Habsburg Family had been marrying cousins for centuries, while they had ruled Europe until the 18th century. Why was it immoral for House Beaumont to be the 21st-century equivalent?

Pierre wiped his nose; this was his ultimate goal. The Beaumonts were destined to rule the world. Yet, to reach that goal, he would need to find a replicated Zeto Crystal, revive Martin Orchard, and convince him to unlock the late Ben Yehuda's Zetan Monocle so Delphine could wear it.

Pierre picked up his phone and called Vladimir. There was no response and Pierre felt how his chest got tighter. He felt terrified that Vladimir would abandon him because of their trivial fight. If Vladimir abandoned Pierre, how could he ever achieve his goal of world dominance?

As Pierre watched the sun setting behind the mountains, he decided to go inside, have a nap, and clear his mind of his troubles.

"WAKE UP, DELPHINE. Your time has come."

Delphine Beaumont woke up with a twitch, as a harrowing voice was echoing in the back of her head. "What time is it?" Delphine asked the room's AI, but there was no response. How peculiar. Delphine heard how the door to her room unlocked, and she had a flashback from her passionate encounter with Lucien just a few nights earlier. As she came, her mind had elevated and she had spotted a tiny hidden camera in the room. When she came back to her senses from the exhilarating experience, she had been unable to find the camera. Yet she knew that Constance had been spying on her.

Delphine looked at the door. No-one was entering but she was certain she had heard the door unlock. Was Constance testing her?

Thinking of Constance, Delphine reflected that she hadn't seen her tormentor for two days. It was unusual for Constance to have days off, as her aging tormentor had nothing else to live for.

"Go Delphine. Your time has come." A voice echoed again. "Who are you?" Delphine asked, but there was only silence.

Delphine realised that it was past midnight and it was a Monday. She remembered the terrifying creature that appeared in the mirror, Empress Rangda

Kaliankan, who had told her to seduce her brother and kill all of her siblings and her father. The very same creature had told her that tonight was the night she would kill her father and her siblings to become the true heir to the Beaumont family.

Delphine got to her wardrobe and got dressed in sturdy clothes, suitable for combat. Tonight, she wouldn't be a princess, tonight she would be a warrior, ready to take what was hers. She opened the door and snuck into the empty corridor, ready to convince her brother to join her.

LUCIEN STARED AT DELPHINE in shock as she put her hand over his mouth and spoke:

- Shh! Don't be afraid, Lucien. Tonight is the night we fulfil our destiny.

Lucien nodded, and Delphine removed her hand so Lucien could reply:

- Have you come to seduce me again, Delphine?

Delphine shook her head and replied:

- No. As much as I yearn for your body, tonight is about something much more important. We need to kill our siblings and our father. It is time for us to rule House Beaumont and the world. As brother and sister. As husband and wife.

Lucien:

- Is there no other way? I also hate our father, but our siblings are innocent.

Delphine:

- This is the only way. Once our father is dead, there will be a fight about his inheritance. The only way to avoid it is if we are the only ones remaining. If we don't kill the others, one of them will kill us. She has shown it to me.

Lucien:

- Who is she?

Delphine:

- Empress Rangda Kaliankan of the Xenos.

As Delphine mentioned Rangda's name, her eyes were flashing purple. Lucien flinched and stuttered:

- D...D..D..D... Delphine! what's happening to your eyes?!

Delphine:

- She is showing us the path to glory. Either you follow me on my path to magnificence, or you'll die here with the others.

Lucien:

- Very well. Lead the way, sister.

Delphine nodded, kissed Lucien, and hurried towards the guardhouse for the first step of her plan.

RODOLPHE BERGER WAS struggling to stay awake in the security office of the Beaumont Heritage Centre. The last few days had been stressful, since the head supervisor of the facility, superintendent Constance Monet, had died in a mysterious traffic accident. Rodolphe Berger felt uneasy and he wanted to quit his job. Yet, he knew the risks of quitting on Pierre and his terrifying associate, Vladimir Kravchenko. This conundrum had kept him awake for several days after Constance's death. During the night, Rodolphe couldn't stay awake any longer and he dozed off.

Rodolphe woke up as he was gasping for air. Not until it was too late, did he realise that he was under attack, as Delphine suffocated him from behind with one of Lucien's neck ties.

AFTER ELIMINATING THE security guard, Delphine grabbed his gun and rushed ahead to the boiler room of the Beaumont Heritage Centre. She ran fast and silent like a tiger, and Lucien struggled to keep up with her. Delphine used Rodolphe's security pass to enter the room, and she tampered with the boiler to cause a delayed explosion. After that, she rushed towards the corridor where her siblings lived. As the fire alarm went off, the doors unlocked and Delphine shot everyone who left their rooms with lethal precision. When the fire became too intense, she exclaimed:

- Let's leave, Lucien. Let our siblings choke and burn.

Shocked and fazed from seeing Delphine murder her siblings, Lucien didn't object and he followed her in a trance-like state, amazed at her sudden prowess and strength.

Delphine and Lucien reached the courtyard. Delphine stole the deceased Rodolphe's car, and she programmed it to travel to Palace Beaumont, to settle the score with Pierre. After that, she jumped on her brother and seduced him while the car was on auto-drive mode.

Chapter 5: The Beaumont Family Showdown, 7th November 2039.

Pierre Beaumont woke up as his monocle was beeping loudly to warn him of danger. He inserted it into his right eye, and it showed him a video feed from Rodolphe's car. Delphine and Lucien were copulating, and they would arrive at Palace Beaumont in fifteen minutes. Pierre turned off the video. As much as he wanted to watch them going at it, the fact they were heading towards him in a stolen car could only mean one thing, something disastrous had happened at the Beaumont Heritage Centre.

Pierre tried connecting to the security cameras at the facility centre, but the AI had malfunctioned and wouldn't let him access them. Instead, Pierre connected to a nearby traffic camera, and he deduced that the heritage centre was on fire. Pierre realised what this meant, Delphine was making a move towards seizing power, and she had gotten rid of her rivals to his inheritance.

Pierre screamed out a shocked cry. If he was correct, 22 out of his 24 children were dead. While it was one of the scenarios he had thought of in the past, he had hoped for a more cordial fate among his children.

Pierre called Sergei, one of his bodyguards, and spoke:

- I have visitors coming. Stay out of their way and let them into the palace.

Sergei:

- What about you, Mr Beaumont. Should we lead you to safety?

Pierre:

- No, I will be waiting in the reading room. This is a Beaumont Family matter that I need to deal with myself.

Pierre watched the CCTV videos as his guards hurried to take cover. It had come to this. If he could convince Delphine to join him, they could rule the world together, if not, he would punish her for killing his other progeny.

Pierre made his way to the reading room and poured himself a glass of Cognac. He got seated in a couch and he told the AI to set the music to Hector Berlioz - Dream of a Witches' Sabbath.

PIERRE SMILED CROOKEDLY as he saw his children Delphine and Lucien approach him in the reading room. Delphine was aiming a pistol at him. He turned off the music and spoke:

- Welcome, my children. Apologies for the lack of hospitality options. It's a work health and safety issue.

Delphine:

- What are you talking about, Father? Where are the rest of the people in the palace?

Pierre:

- I can't risk the wellbeing of my employees when my murderous children are visiting.

Delphine:

- So, you know why we are here?

Pierre:

- Of course. While I predicted this outcome in one of my scenarios, I am still disappointed. You could have achieved more if you cooperated with your siblings, instead of killing them, Delphine.

- Yet, killing me won't achieve anything. I have given Raphael access to my hidden bank accounts and he will inherit my estate. You two, on the other hand, will go to prison for murder of the Beaumont offspring. Unless Raphael sends Vladimir, to put you out of your misery, you will be in prison for life.

Lucien:

- Shut up! I don't believe you at all!

Pierre:

- Yet you know that I am telling the truth, Lucien. You shouldn't have followed your sister. However, I understand you. I felt the same way for my sister when I was young. Unfortunately, she died before I reached puberty, so I could never act on my desire.

Lucien:

- Fuck off. You don't know what you are talking about.

Pierre:

- But I do.

Having said this, Pierre snapped his fingers and a hologram video of Lucien and Delphine engaging in coitus appeared in the room. Pierre studied his progeny. The monocle determined Lucien to be a high threat, while Delphine was ambivalent. This suited Pierre. He needed Delphine to be his heir, while the loss of Lucien's life, was in the grand scheme of things, irrelevant.

Pierre:

- The affection you feel for your sister is perfectly natural, Lucien. The Egyptian pharaohs procreated with their siblings and they created the pyramids. The Hapsburgs married their cousins, and they ruled Europe for centuries. The Beaumonts can do it and rule the world.

Delphine interjected:

- We didn't come to seek your approval. We came to take your place. Where is Raphael?

Pierre:

- Do you think ignorance took me to my position?
- I'd be a fool if I told you.

Lucien:

- I don't care. All I see is a defenceless frail old man who is losing his edge!

Pierre:

- Oh, but is that so?

- I let the two of you in, and my bodyguards will kill you if any harm comes to me.

Pierre turned to Delphine:

- I will let you in on the family business and I'll give you the technology that made me the wealthiest man in the world. However, you need to be punished. Kill Lucien. The two of you need to suffer for what you did to my other children.

Pierre took out Ben Yehuda's monocle from his pocket and spoke again:

- This monocle contains an advanced alien AI. If you wear it, you can rule the world, Delphine. Kill your brother.

Delphine:

- Or we can take it off your dead body.

Delphine turned to Lucien and spoke:

- Lucien, seize the monocles from our father.

Lucien walked up to Pierre and try to pull the monocle off Pierre's face. Lucien shouted in pain and stumbled backwards as the monocle electrocuted him. Pierre laughed menacingly and continued:

- Tsk, Tsk. The monocle cannot be taken, it can only be given.

Hearing this, Delphine fired the pistol and hit the couch Pierre was sitting in, just below his crotch. Delphine shouted:

- Then give us the bloody monocle or we'll make your death excruciating.

Pierre sighed and realised that as much as he wanted the Beaumonts to rule the world, he was even keener on securing his own survival. He nodded, tapped on the top of his monocle to remove it, and he threw it to Delphine.
Delphine laughed and replied:

- That's it. Give us your real monocle instead of the booby-trapped one! Now let's find out what this one does.

Having said this, Delphine put on the monocle and as is it connected with her mind, she felt amazing. She felt so much sharper and so alert, she felt higher than a normal human, she felt like a goddess.
Meanwhile, Pierre was counting the seconds. When the anti-theft property of the monocle activated, he threw himself to the ground and pulled out the pistol that he had strapped to the bottom of the couch. Lucien saw what was

about to happen, and ran towards Pierre. A shot went off, and Pierre passed out as the force from Lucien's kick smashed him in the face.

"MR BEAUMONT, WHAT HAPPENED here?"

Pierre woke up with blood stinging in his eyes, nostrils, and mouth. He looked at his bodyguards Sergei and Vitali and replied:

- I had a problem with my children. Are any of them alive?

Sergei shook his head and replied:

- The boy, you shot him through the heart. The girl... It looks like the monocle drilled through her brain.

Hearing this, Pierre crawled over to Delphine's corpse, deactivated her monocle and inserted it into his eye. He took a deep breath of relief when the alien AI reconnected with his mind. The monocle was operational and he could still salvage this situation. Pierre turned to Sergei and spoke:

- Take the bodies of my children to the cryogenic tanks in my research lab.

Sergei nodded and replied:

- And what about you, sir?

Pierre:

- I will contact my medical experts. Any news about Vladimir Kravchenko?

Sergei:

- No. We haven't heard from our master in a few days. Should we keep looking?

Pierre:

- Yes. I need to speak to him. Now more than ever.

Sergei:

- Understood, Pierre. We will carry out your mission.

Pierre left the room without a word. His broken nose pained him, but not as much as the loss of his progeny. He hoped Vladimir would get back to him, because without Vladimir, there was no way for him to sort out this mess, and he might as well end everything.

Chapter 6: The Beaumont's must rise again. 12th November 2039

"I don't know anything about the tragedy at my boarding school for gifted children."

Pierre Beaumont felt stressed as he sat in a police interrogation room in Geneva. While the police were powerless to prosecute him due to his power over the Swiss government, the police investigation still impeded his plans. Instead of being cryogenically frozen in his research lab, the majority of his progeny were in the mortuary and would most likely receive a funeral.

Crime Inspector Cherise Villeneuve turned to Pierre and spoke:

- So, tell me Monsieur Beaumont. How come all of these children bear your family name.

Pierre:

- Because I adopted them all. Legally, they are all my children.

Cherise:

- Hmmm. They were all born the same year, 2023, and you adopted all of them at birth according to the legal papers. But do tell me Monsieur Beaumont, how did you know they were gifted if you adopted them at birth?

Pierre:

- I did not per se. However, the development potential in children increases through the power of positive affirmation. Thus, by calling the children gifted, I wanted to fill them with pride in their abilities.

Cherise:

- I see.
- What can you tell me about the mothers of these children?

Pierre:

- I assume they had their reasons for not wanting to raise their children. I didn't question their motives for putting their children up for adoption.

Cherise:

- Why did you decide to adopt 24 children?

Pierre:

- I wanted to give more children the chance of good schooling. The Beaumont Foundation is donating money to charitable projects all over the world, but I wanted to follow this group more closely. In any case, I don't see how this have any relevance to the investigation?

Cherise:

- It is very relevant to our investigation. Our forensic investigation concluded that all the children at the facility were siblings. Furthermore, their genetic markers were closer than average siblings, as if they were products of incest.

Hearing this, Pierre felt how panic was engulfing him. He had got away with many of his crimes against humanity, but would his top-secret breeding program be the end of him? He wanted to lawyer up and refuse to answer more questions, but he also wanted to talk his way out of trouble, like he had done many times in the past.

Pierre:

- That is impossible, I urge you to get an independent genetics lab to redo the genetic sampling.

Cherise:

- Yes, we have that on our agenda.

Pierre:

- I see. I would suggest you don't publicise your findings until you have performed an independent audit. I would rather avoid fruitless conspiracy theories risking the good work of the Beaumont Foundation and the World Bank.

Cherise:

- Of course. The Swiss government has classified the investigation for now.

Pierre:

- Good. Now if you excuse me, I need to leave. I must deal with the aftermath of this tragedy.

Cherise looked at Pierre and an awkward silence occurred. Eventually, Crime Inspector Cherise conceded and spoke:

- Okay, Pierre. We will be in touch in regards to this critical investigation. Au revoir.

Pierre didn't reply, grabbed his suitcase, and hurried to leave the police station.

"LE PDG DE LA BANQUE Mondiale emmené au commissariat de police après les morts mystérieuses au Centre du Patrimoine de Beaumont." ("The CEO of the World Bank, Pierre Beaumont, taken to the police station after the mysterious deaths of numerous children at the Beaumont Heritage Centre")

Pierre put down the tablet after reading an article including a photograph of himself at the Geneva police station. Pierre hated the independent press and that he could not completely control the flow of information, despite having power of the news and social media. Crime Inspector Cherise Villeneuve was a nuisance, and he should have crushed her by now, but instead, he felt weary and low. A few weeks earlier, he had anticipated a great future for House Beaumont, and yet here he was, an aging man, being the sole survivor of his great house.

Pierre walked out on his terrace and he overlooked the beautiful valley below. Normally, it would give him solace, but as he watched the steep fall on the other side of the ledge, he wanted to end it all. This was it. This was how the greatest man who had ever walked upon the planet would end his days, hated and alone after murdering his children in self-defence.

Pierre looked at the valley below. Should he write a suicide letter, exposing the crimes of the Monocle Conspiracy? He decided against it. Humans were sheep and they deserved to suffer for their weakness and stupidity. Allowing his co-conspirators to carry on with their schemes was the least he could do against the rotten masses that existed to serve him.

"Adieu la vie cruelle. Puissions-nous nous revoir, Delphine, mon amour." (Goodbye cruel life. May we meet again, Delphine, my love.) Pierre mumbled as he climbed over the edge and fell towards the valley below. 20 seconds of freefalling and it would be over.

After freefalling for several seconds, Pierre twitched as someone grabbed him mid-air and he felt the sudden deceleration from an opening parachute.

"You cannot kill yourself; you are mine to kill!" Vladimir yelled.

The duo landed relatively unscathed, although Pierre strained his ankle upon landing.

Pierre whined:

- Oh, mon Dieu. My ankle. That hurts a lot.

Vladimir taunted:

- Did it hurt more than breaking every bone in your body while bleeding out on the ground?

Pierre:

- I wouldn't know.
- What happened? Where did you come from?

Vladimir:

- I have been watching you since our fight, Pierre.

Pierre:

- How did you evade my guards and my building security?

Vladimir:

- I stole a personal cloaking device from the Harapan Conglomerate a while back. It's developed from Zetan technology.

Pierre:

- Bloody hell. Why didn't you tell me?

Vladimir:

- Because it was more fun not telling you.

- Anyways, you cannot die yet. The Beaumont's must rise again. I can't wait to see the mayhem Lucien and Delphine will unleash onto this world.

Pierre:

- But they are dead, and besides, the police are on to me.

Vladimir:

- The primordial Zeto Crystal can bring them back. I have already dealt with Cherise Villeneuve.

Pierre:

- Bah. I doubt killing Cherise will help me with my current predicament.

Vladimir:

- That's why I didn't kill her. Instead, I forged evidence that Cherise was a member of a conspiracy group that obsessed about you. To add some spice to her profile, I also faked evidence that she was involved with the Geneva Hei Bai virus outbreak that occurred last year.

Pierre:

- Oh, Vladimir. I don't know how to thank you. I am sorry about our silly fight after you murdered Constance Monet.

Vladimir:

- Apology accepted. Let's get back to Palace Beaumont and rest.

After saying this, Vladimir carried Pierre to a nearby road, and from there, they ordered a self-driving cab that took them back to Palace Beaumont, where they pursued a crazy night of romping and sadistic sex rituals.

Chapter 7: We must revive Martin Orchard and reclaim the primordial Zeto Crystal from Sabina Hines, 12th December 2039.

Pierre Beaumont was enjoying a glass of cognac in his top-secret research lab. The last month had been a monumental success due to Vladimir's faithful help, and Pierre questioned why he had ever fought with his long-time lover and partner in crime.

Cherise Villeneuve had been taken off the investigation on the mysterious deaths at the Beaumont Heritage Centre. Instead, the Swiss Government had appointed a politruk to oversee the investigation. As expected, he hadn't found anything that implicated Pierre. Instead, the blame for the murders had befallen an Islamic terrorist group that was an enemy of the World Bank.

Pierre had covered up that the children were his biological children conceived through incest, by having his associate Josefina Fiero purchase the laboratory and falsify the results. Remaining a free man, Pierre had got access to his dead children's bodies and he had staged a funeral. Their charred bodies remained in cryogenic preservation, waiting for Pierre to get hold of the primordial Zeto Crystal so he could revive them.

Vladimir Kravchenko entered the facility and approached Pierre. Vladimir:

- It seems that everything is under control. We should do our part to revive Delphine.

Pierre:

- Yes.

- Did you know that it was Martin Orchard's daughter, Sabina Hines, who convinced Martin to kill Ben Yehuda and help her steal the primordial Zeto Crystal in the Solomon temple?

Vladimir:

- Yes, but what does it matter to us? All we need to do is figure out where Sabina is hiding the crystal, and take it from her.

Pierre:

- No.

- I believe Ben Yehuda was on to something. The day before he died, he claimed that Sabina was a touch empath.

Vladimir:

- A touch empath? What the hell is that?

Pierre:

- According to legend, a person able to influence others through the power of touch.

Vladimir:

- Why do I care?

Pierre:

- Because we are dealing with a very powerful entity. When she was 18, Sabina travelled to Jerusalem by herself, met up with Martin, opened the ancient gate of the Templar Tunnels, and stole the Zeto Crystal in front of our eyes. Now at the age of 20, she is incredibly rich and influential. It would be unwise to put ourself on a confrontation course with Sabina.

Vladimir:

- So, what do you suggest?

Pierre:

- We should revive Martin Orchard and implant him with a remote-controlled nerve-pain-amplifier. That will make him our slave. We can use Martin's paternal relationship to Sabina to find out where she is hiding the primordial Zeto Crystal without confronting her ourselves.

Vladimir:

- Very well. So, where do we get the next replicated Zeto Crystal?

Pierre:

- The next Zetan temple that will be open is the Shankaracharya temple in Kashmir. It will be possible to open from midnight to dawn on the 4th January 2040.

Vladimir:

- Very well. This should be an interesting trip.

Pierre:

- Yes. I am coming with you.

Vladimir:

- Really? You have not been to a Zetan Temple since the incident in Colombia in the year 2026.

Pierre:

- Incorrect. I did go to the Templar Tunnels in 2029. In any case, this is about the future of House Beaumont. I cannot leave it to others.

Vladimir:

  - Very well.
  - I'll make the arrangements and I'll find a suitable crew.

Pierre:

  - I am glad to have you, Vladimir.

After saying this, Pierre walked up to Vladimir and kissed him with a passion he hadn't experienced in decades.

Chapter 8: Jared Pond, no longer a sex god. 24th December 2039

Jared Pond was sitting at a poker table at Crown Casino in Sydney. While his nick for poker was there, so much else had changed. He had lost his penchant for danger, booze, beautiful women, and he spent most of his days thinking about what could have been. He regretted that he broke up with the beautiful Eileen Lu, his one true love, back in 2023.

Jared Pond had never liked the spotlight he received from being the first gentleman to Eileen, who became the interim president of China after the collapse of the Columnist Party in 2021. At the time, he had convinced himself that he disliked the new policies that Eileen proposed. However, the whole debacle was about something else. Jared couldn't handle living in the shadow of his much more successful partner.

After the break-up, Jared's career as a field agent for the Royal Australian Kangaroo Intelligence (RAKI) was over. He had gained too much fame during his years as the first gentleman in China to be able to do reconnaissance in the field. Instead, he had focused on his poker playing and drinking, while occasionally doing some consultation work with RAKI. No longer doing fieldwork, Jared had turned rather plump, and this is in combination with the merciless effect of aging, had turned him into anything but a sex god.

Jared found himself stalking Eileen's social media account from his phone, and he realised that enough was enough. He needed to flirt with some fresh exotic women to get over his memory-induced melancholy.

Jared collected his poker winnings and he transferred them to his bank account. After that, he walked to a table where a few good sorts were drinking and gossiping.

Jared:

- The name is Pond, Jared Pond.

Bimbo:

- Who asked you, grandpa?

As the Bimbo turned to her friends and laughed, Jared decided to move on. He wasn't here to teach young women about proper manners. In any case, that would be a ridiculous proposition, since he had tried picking up a woman 30 years his junior. Jared walked to the bar and ordered a double scotch. An Eastern European woman approached him and spoke:

- Well played at the poker table, Mr Pond. I'll be yours for the night for 20 pineapples.

In his intoxicated state, Jared missed out on the $2000 price tag. Instead, he only heard the part about how his great poker playing made him irresistible to the semi-attractive lady. Jared smiled and replied:

- I love your enthusiasm, Ms....?

Woman:

- Svetlana Antonov, but you can call me Foxy.

Jared:

- Very well, Foxy. I accept your offer to spend the night. Please accompany me to room 7007. We'll keep the champagne cool and everything else hot.

After saying this, Foxy accompanied Jared to his room and they spent the night experiencing Jared's talent for lovemaking.

THE NEXT MORNING, JARED woke up full of confidence. How silly of him to spend time self-pitying and stalking his ex on social media, when he could pick up Russian bombshells half his age.

Jared tapped Foxy's shoulder and smiled as she opened her eyes. Jared spoke:

- Good morning, beautiful. Are you ready for another round of the Pond-train?

Foxy mumbled and replied:

- Sure, if you give me another five pineapples.

After that, she closed her eyes and fell back into slumber.

Foxy's response confused Jared. Why on Earth did she ask for pineapples? Could the woman be a prostitute?

Jared concluded that he was a sex god who wouldn't need to pay a woman of the night to get laid. Thus, Foxy's request for pineapples had to be for actual pineapples, five pineapples to be precise. He picked up the phone and called room service:

- Hello. I would like to order five pineapples to room 7007.

Waiter:

- Would you like them cut or whole?

Jared hadn't anticipated this question, as no one had ever asked him for pineapples after coitus before, so he replied:

- Cut half of them and bring the rest whole.

Waiter:

- Of course, Mr Pond.

A few minutes later, a waiter knocked on the door and delivered the pineapples.

As the waiter left, Jared smiled and he took a slice of pineapples to Foxy and tapped her on the shoulder. It was time for the Pond-train to have a morning departure. As Foxy woke up, she stared at him in awe and exclaimed:

- Why are you trying to feed me a pineapple, you crazy Australian? I am allergic to pineapples, are you trying to kill me?

Jared:

- How would I know? I hardly know your name. In any case, you asked me for pineapples 15 minutes ago.

Foxy:

- Pineapples, as in $100 bills you moron. I want 20 of them for last night.

Jared:

- What? I am not going to pay you! The sex was a privilege for you.

Foxy:

- You are an idiot!

Having said this, Foxy grabbed her stuff and stormed out of Jared's room.

JARED WAS REFLECTING over last night's events when there was a knock on the door. Foxy had returned, accompanied by two Russian goons. One of them spoke:

- Hey Mr Pond. Pay Roxy what you owe her, or else...

Jared realised that this was exactly the excitement he needed in life. First having sex with a beautiful woman and then knocking out the goons sent to kill him. Jared smiled and replied:

- I choose to fight.

Having said this, Jared swung at the closest Russian, but he shouldn't have. Jared was now past 50 years old and far from his prime. 20 seconds later, Jared lay on the floor after receiving a few knocks to the head.

One of the Russians approached him with a printed invoice and spoke:

- So, Mr Pond. Here is your invoice from today's encounter. $20,000. $2000 for the night with Roxy, $2000 for our callout fee, and $16000 to fix Alexis' missing tooth. Pay within seven days or we'll take you to court.

Jared:

- Wait, you came here to fight me and now you're threatening me with a lawsuit? What kind of Russians are you?!

Alexis:

- We are legitimate businessmen in the adult entertainment industry, who came here to deliver an invoice since you refused to pay Roxy as agreed. You were the one who resorted to violence, Mr Pond.

Jared:

- Very well. I'll speak to my accountant and I'll organise the payment of your invoice.

Alexis:

- Thank you. Please call our 24-hour-hotline if you have any questions. The number is on the invoice.

- Do svidaniya, mister Pond.

As the Russians left the room, Jared sighed. How had he, the greatest Australian secret agent to ever walk the earth, turned into a John who got knocked out while fighting debt collectors? Time and aging were indeed merciless beasts.

Chapter 9: Jared Pond receives a mission to investigate Pierre's actions in India. 28th December 2039

The prime minister of Australia, Danielle Anders, were throwing darts at a picture of Pierre Beaumont. She was mad at her former benefactor, who had helped her rigging the Australian elections the previous year. Pierre had refused to pay Danielle her Christmas bonus for 2039, and when she finally got hold of him, he had mocked her with these words:

"Why would I bribe the puppet who I helped rise to power? Setting you up as the prime minister was just a game for me, a game where I tested how much I could troll the public. You are, after all, the gender-corrected version of the most hated politician in Australia's history, Danielle, or should I call you Daniel?"

Danielle knew that Pierre was a terrifying opponent and she needed to dig up dirt on him. The signal-tracking from her phone call with Pierre showed that Pierre was in the contested Kashmir region of India. This was not part of his official itinerary and Danielle knew that he was up to something illegitimate. If she could find evidence against Pierre, she could blackmail him to avoid having her secret revealed.

But who would she send? It would be too obvious if she sent RAKI operatives to Kashmir. If she did, Pierre would know that she had betrayed him and he would use his powers over the media and corporate world to hang her out dry. But what about sending that old fool Jared Pond? He had stopped being a RAKI operative after his relationship with Eileen Lu back in 2021 had made him too famous to make him a viable field agent. Sending Jared would be unexpected, so Pierre couldn't anticipate that she was behind it if Jared got caught.

Danielle picked up the phone and summoned Jared to the Kirribilli House, the Sydney residence for the Australian Prime Minister.

JARED POND WAS FEELING confused and sweaty in his Sydney apartment. It was a muggy day, the air-conditioning of his unit was broken, and he still had a headache from getting knocked out three days earlier. Worst of all were those police officers who had come to his place to interview him. The Russian debt collectors he had fought at Crown Casino had filed charges against him as they had photographic evidence that he started the fight. How had life come to this? How could Australia's greatest agent be charged after losing a fight to a group of shady Russians?

Ring, Ring

Jared Pond stared in disbelief when his phone showed an incoming call from Prime Minister Danielle Anders. Jared yelped and answered the phone:

- Hello, Daniel! How can I be of assistance?

Danielle:

- It's Danielle these days, and I would appreciate it if you got it right.

Jared sighed and replied:

- Oh, yes! Hello, Danielle. What do you want from me?

Danielle:

- I am summoning you to Kirribilli House. Be there in two hours.

Jared:

- There is a slight problem with that request. I have literally no desire to meet you.

Danielle:

- Tsk, tsk, tsk.

- I guess I'll just ask the police to stall the Crown Casino incident investigation. In the meantime, you'll be banned from leaving Sydney and barred from all licensed venues. Yes, that's right. No more poker for you, Jared.

Jared:

- Okay. I will be there in two hours.

Danielle:

- Excellent. I can't wait to meet with one of the legends of our intelligence community. Make sure to freshen up and dress well. You are meeting with the Prime Minister after all.

Jared hung up and went to the bathroom to take a cold shower. This day was on the trajectory to be really rotten.

DANIELLE SMIRKED AS Jared entered her office. Seeing her smirk, Jared got reminded of a previous incident. He had played a poker tournament at Mount Druitt RSL and he had woken up next to a woman with a similar smirk. Had that woman also been a man? This thought, combined with alcohol withdrawal and untreated concussion made Jared vomit in his mouth, and he rushed off to the toilet.

As he returned to the Prime Minister's office, Danielle spoke:

- So, is this the fate that has befallen the once-great Jared Pond, a drunk who vomits in the Prime Minister's bathroom?

Jared:

- Cut to the chase, Danielle. I am only here to find out what I need to do to avoid an indefinite and unjustified police investigation.

Danielle handed Jared a photograph of Pierre Beaumont and spoke:

- Pierre Beaumont. My sources tell me that he is in the Kashmir region of India. I want you to find out what he is doing there.

Jared:

- What on earth does this have to do with Australian state affairs?

Danielle:

- It got nothing to do with Australia. It's a personal issue between me and Pierre, which is why I am sending a washed-up former agent instead of sending one of RAKI's top agents.

Jared:

- Why?

Danielle:

- Plausible deniability. Who would believe that I sent a washed-up former agent if things go south?

Jared:

- So, what's in it for me?

Danielle:

- I'll make sure that the police drop the charges against you for the Crown Casino incident.

- I also have crucial information regarding your old flame, Eileen Lu. Her life is in danger, and helping me is the only way for you to save her.

Jared:

- You're bluffing!

Danielle:

- Perhaps, but are you willing to take the risk?

Jared sighed. He hated Danielle Anders for figuring out that Eileen still was his weakness after all these years. But what would he do? He could refuse, but then Danielle would ban him from living any form of life for the foreseeable future. Besides, he did miss the sensation of being on a mission.
Jared:

- So, what would you have me do?

Danielle handed Jared a flight itinerary and spoke:

- The flight to Delhi departs tonight. From there you'll take a local flight to Kashmir. My trace on Pierre's phone call indicated that he is close to the Shankaracharya temple. Go there and find out what is up to. Be wary, your old friend Vladimir Kravchenko will be nearby.

Jared:

- Just the man I wanted to meet!

Danielle:

- He did save you from Jing Xi's captivity and certain death. Now leave my office, Jared. I can't handle the odour that is coming from your mouth.

Having said this, Danielle pressed a button and summoned two body-guards who confiscated Jared's phone and issued him with a new one. After that, they led him out of the office.

Chapter 10: Pierre secures a replicated Zeto Crystal and Vladimir captures Jared Pond. 4th January 2040

Pierre was enjoying the icy mountain winds that struck his face while he was waiting for the secret passageway at the Shankaracharya temple to open. The cold winds reminded him of the winters in Switzerland and it was far superior to the muggy heat which he had endured while meeting with various dignitaries in India. Pierre used his Zetan Monocle to do an infrared sweep of the surroundings. He had paid off the police to make a perimeter and keep away from the temple, but one could never be too careful.

Much to his dismay, Pierre's monocle detected a man in hiding, 500 metres away. The man was also equipped with an infrared camera. Pierre shouted to Vladimir:

- Vladimir. Come here!

Vladimir approached Pierre who spoke:

- Vladimir! A man is spying on us over there. The chief of police has betrayed us.

Vladimir laughed and replied:

- That's nothing to worry about. That's just the washed-up Australian ex-agent, Jared Pond.

Pierre stared at Vladimir and spoke:

- How long have you known about this?

Vladimir:

- He has been following us for days. Probably on the orders from your mistress, Danielle Anders. Let him watch. He'll be dead soon anyway.

Pierre whinged:

- Why haven't you told me, and what have you planned for Jared Pond?

Vladimir shrugged his shoulders and replied:

- I wanted to see how long it would take for you to notice it.
- You are getting very slow.

Pierre:

- Don't you dare to question my abilities. Hmmph!

Vladimir:

- Improve your performance and I won't have to.
- No matter, it's midnight and it's time to get that bloody crystal.

Pierre:

- What about Jared Pond?

Vladimir:

- As I said, I'll deal with it.

Having said this, Vladimir pulled a lever in the temple, and the whole wall lit up with bluish alien symbols. Vladimir's monocle gave him the secret code and he tapped the symbols in the correct order. This opened a secret door.

Vladimir ventured through the door with Pierre in tow and they entered the inner sanctum of the temple.

JARED LOOKED IN AMAZEMENT as the wall lit up with alien symbols after Vladimir pulled the lever. How had this happened and why had no-one ever discovered these strange symbols before? Jared tried taking a few photos from afar, but he couldn't get a clear shot. He hesitated for a moment. Did he want to disturb the volatile and dangerous Vladimir Kravchenko who was up to something? A part of him wanted to run away, but then he remembered Danielle Anders' claim that Eileen Lu was in danger. Jared couldn't let his cowardice endanger Eileen.

As Vladimir and Pierre entered the temple, Jared rushed to the wall to get a better look at the symbols. To his disappointment, the wall was no longer glowing. To make matters worse, he felt a heavy thump in the back of his head, before everything turned black.

"WELCOME TO THE INNER sanctum of the Shankaracharya Temple, Mr Pond."

As Jared Pond opened his eyes, he noticed a glowing blue gemstone surrounded by the darkness of the rest of the temple. Vladimir Kravchenko smirked towards Jared and spoke:

- How do you like the replicated Zeto Crystal, Mr Pond?

Jared:

- I don't know what you are talking about. What is that, and what are you up to here?

Vladimir:

- The replicated Zeto Crystals are marvellous artefacts that were created by the Zetan species. An advanced alien race that altered our human genome and founded our first civilisations. These crystals can even raise the dead.

Pierre interjected:

- Why are you telling the Australian spy our secrets? Have you lost your mind?

Vladimir:

- Because he can join us. We have a slot to fill after Ben Yehuda's death.

Pierre:

- What makes you think you can invite Jared to our group?

Vladimir:

- Because I am the best fighter in our group and the only one with a pistol in this room.

Pierre was about to argue, but he held his tongue, not daring to stir the ire of the unpredictable Vladimir.
Jared:

- I am sorry, but I'll pass on your invitation, Vladimir. Threesomes with aging men have never been on my agenda.

Having said this, Jared tried to sucker punch Vladimir, who acted lightning fast, dodging Jared's punch and then flooring him with a kick to the knee. As Jared collapsed to the ground, Vladimir taunted.

- This wasn't an invite. It was a demand. However, I am in a good mood, so if you pick up the crystal and hand it to me, I won't kill you.

Jared realised that there was no point in keep getting knocked out from arguing with Russians. He complied with Vladimir's request and took the replicated Zeto Crystal from the plinth and handed it to Vladimir. As this occurred, Vladimir and Pierre looked tense for a few seconds until Vladimir exhaled, and laughed a burst of roaring laughter.

- You did it, Jared. Welcome to the group.

Vladimir's statement confused Jared and he replied:

- I did what exactly?

Vladimir:

- You did something amazing. Let's leave this place so we can celebrate.

Having said this, Vladimir and Pierre left the room and Jared tentatively followed them. He thought about trying to sucker punch Vladimir, but he refrained from doing so, as he wanted to avoid embarrassing himself by copping another beating.

As they left the temple, Vladimir turned around and knocked Jared unconscious. Pierre gave him a sceptical look and spoke:

- Can you explain what you are doing, Vladimir?

Vladimir smirked and replied:

- Normally, the person who picks up the replicated Zeto Crystal gets targeted by the sentry drones and gets killed before I manage to disable the drones. That was Jared's intended role. I don't know what happened in this temple.

Pierre:

- I understand. So, what do you have in mind for Jared?

Vladimir:

- A few of my local talents will keep him contained until I figure out what to do with him.

Pierre:

- I don't like that idea. Jared is a government agent. He might escape and cause trouble.

Vladimir:

- Don't worry about that. Jared is a has-been. He is nothing that Rajesh and Prakash can't handle. Now let's head back to Switzerland so we can bring Martin Orchard back to life. It is time for that bastard to start being useful.

Having said this, Vladimir closed the secret temple-entrance, tied the unconscious Jared to a railing, and called his associates for immediate extraction.

Chapter 11: Jared Pond escapes India. 11th January 2040

J ared Pond was not enjoying himself, as he was chained to the boiler in a dodgy shed, located somewhere in the Kashmiri wilderness. His captors were playing a cruel game on Jared. If the boiler was not on, Jared would freeze to death as the shed would reach the freezing temperatures outside. If the boiler was on, however, Jared would overheat due to being chained to the heating element.

The worst part of his captivity was the confusion that Jared felt. Why had Vladimir ordered his goons to keep Jared as a prisoner? He would understand if Vladimir wanted him dead, but what use was he to the villains alive?

Jared got some clarity to Vladimir's motives when a plump Asian man with a screechy high-pitched voice entered the shed. Jared recognised the man from his pathetic social media stalking sessions of Eileen. The visitor was Peng Yingxing, a Chinese businessman based in Dubai, who was Eileen's current husband. Peng walked up to Jared and spoke:

- Oh, the famous Jared Pond. How I have waited for this moment to happen.

Jared:

- Why? Is this a sexual fantasy of yours?

Peng punched Jared in the face, and Jared didn't flinch as Peng was much weaker than the henchmen that usually punched Jared. Peng gave him a disappointed look and spoke:

- You continue to insult me, Mr Pond, but I will get the last laugh.

Jared:

- I am not following you. Have our paths ever crossed?

Peng:

- You ruined Eileen for me. Whatever I do, I am not good enough at sex for her. This is your fault.

Jared:

- Thanks.

- Yes, bedroom activities have always been my strength. But why did you come all the way here to whine about your sexual inadequacy?

Peng:

- Don't flatter yourself. I came to oversee my opium smuggling business when Rajesh and Prakash revealed that they held you as a captive for Vladimir Kravchenko. I am paying them the double amount to kill you instead of keeping you as a prisoner. Thus, I will finally be able to kill the ghost from Eileen's past that has haunted me.

Jared:

- Viagra. The secret is Viagra.

Peng punched Jared again, this time with enough force to draw blood.

- I will kill you for your insolence, Guay-lo.

Jared:

- Oh well. Best of luck with Vladimir Kravchenko, I suppose.

Hearing this, Peng muttered something and stormed off.

Jared watched Peng as he left, and he sighed to himself. How could life have come to this? He would be murdered on the orders of a pathetic creature who couldn't compete with him for Eileen's favour. On the flipside, if he got out of this mess alive, there was still a chance to rekindle the flame with Eileen.

THE FOLLOWING DAY, the Indian henchmen Rajesh and Prakash entered the shed. They argued in Hindi and Jared heard them mentioning Vladimir several times. Jared presumed that they debated whether it was wise to double-cross the deadliest assassin in history to double their pay. Jared concluded that it wasn't. A much wiser option would be to not double-cross Vladimir and bet whatever he paid on red at the casino. That option entailed a 46 % chance of doubling the money and a 0 % chance of getting brutally murdered. After concluding their argument Prakash aimed his pistol towards Jared and Rajesh spoke:

- Mr Pond. Come with us.

Jared:

- I'd rather not. There is a blizzard outside, and after seven days you dimwits have finally set this shed to a comfortable temperature.

Boom
Jared flinched as Prakash shot next to him and threatened:

- Come now. I don't like asking twice.

Jared:

- I hate to be a letdown, but you do realise that I am handcuffed to the boiler.

Prakash nodded to Rajesh, who uncuffed Jared. Jared knew that he needed to time a daring escape, but he hesitated. He had lost his last two fights, and against gun-toting adversaries, a third loss could be his last.

Not feeling that the moment was right, Jared obliged and walked outside the shed with his captors. They walked into a forest grove and they reached a secluded spot. Prakash and Rajesh stopped. Rajesh threw a shovel in front of Jared and spoke:

- There are two types of men in the world. Those with a gun, and those that are digging.

'What kind of idiotic assassin expects his victim to dig a grave when the ground is frozen?' Jared thought and realised that this was his opportunity. He pretended to dig but the shovel couldn't break the ground. Rajesh got closer to him and shouted:

- Dig faster, Australian dog!

'Now!' Jared thought and swung the shovel, hitting Rajesh in the head. As the Indian henchman went down, Jared exclaimed "FOUR!" referring to the cricket term for a good hit. A minor issue remained, Prakash was outside of Jared's range, and he raised his pistol to shoot Jared. 'Please God, give me a six!' Jared mumbled, closed his eyes, and swung the shovel.

A shot went off, and then Jared opened his eyes. He stared at Prakash in disbelief. Against all the odds, Jared had swung the shovel in the way of the bullet from Prakash's pistol. This had caused the bullet to ricochet and hit Prakash in the eye. Jared wasn't about to wait for another miracle, so he rushed to Prakash and kicked him in the head.

After that, he picked up the pistol and left the scene.

JARED WAS SITTING ON an Air India flight to Dubai. He felt a sense of excitement. Not only had he survived an assassination attempt, but he had also found out that Eileen's husband was a drug-dealing scumbag who failed to deliver in the bedroom. This was his chance to save the world yet again, as well as rekindling the long-lost flame with the beautiful Eileen. Satisfied with a good day's work, Jared helped himself to a lot of liquor from the inflight service and fell asleep, dreaming blissful dreams.

Chapter 12: A deadly reunion, 13th January 2040.

E ileen Lu was arranging a flower arrangement at her Dubai mansion for the umpteenth time when a maid approached her and spoke:

- Mistress, we ran out of Jellab and Qamardeen drinks. I fear how your husband will react if he doesn't have a good selection of drinks for the Emir's visit.

Hearing this, Eileen was about to scream in frustration. It was not because of the missing drinks, but that her life had come to this. After she was deposed from the Chinese presidency, the Emir of Dubai had granted her political asylum in Dubai. Unfortunately, this came with some strings attached, and she had reluctantly married the business tycoon Peng Jingxing due to the Emir's insistence. The marriage had been a loveless disaster from the start. Eileen had never liked anything about Peng, neither his looks nor his values. Peng had only married Eileen to improve his status, as it was the height of achievement in some circles to marry the former president. Things hadn't improved after her husband found out that she was unable to conceive. Eileen calmed down and spoke to the servant:

- Mariyah, I trust that you can make a few calls and find a suitable supplier of these beverages. Now leave me alone.

Having said this, Eileen left the reception area and retreated to her private office. She switched on her computer and opened a hidden file containing her autobiography and her political manifesto. Eileen had wanted to publish it for years, but even considering it, would be dangerous. The Columnist Party reigned supreme in China once again, and the Emir of Dubai wasn't a fan of women having political influence.

Eileen closed the file. She was not motivated to write something that she had to hide from the world. She hated her life as a trophy wife to her fat and slimy husband. Eileen closed her eyes, and she wished that she had stayed and fought instead of running away, when the Columnist Party returned to seize power. Even if she had died, it would be better than living in this diminutive existence.

Eileen's phone made a beeping noise and distracted her from her thoughts. She had received a message from Jared Pond. She felt both shocked and excited hearing from him, and although it was dangerous, she couldn't resist the temptation to read his message. The message read:

"Eileen, I need to speak to you. I unveiled some of your husband's dark secrets. Meet me at Zahr El-Laymoun, Downtown Dubai in one hour."

Eileen hesitated for a moment. Could this be her ex-husband Jared? After all these years, why would he contact her again? Or, was it one of her husband's many tests?

'Screw it, I am going!' Eileen said to herself, and felt the excitement and adrenaline from straying from the boring and safe path.

JARED POND WAS DRINKING Jellab (grape juice and rosewater topped with pine nuts) while reflecting over how much better the drink would taste mixed with alcohol. He refrained from finding out. The Dubai government shunned alcohol consumption, and Jared would rather avoid needless confrontation with the Emirati religious police.

He looked up as Eileen approached him cautiously. "Hi, Jared. I'm surprised seeing you here. It has been so many years since we last met."

At first, Eileen's reaction confused him. Hadn't she come to meet him as a friend? But then he realised that she might have people spying on her, and feigning surprise at meeting Jared was for her safety. Jared got up, bowed in front of her, and spoke:

- President Eileen Lu. It's an honour to meet you again.

Eileen:

- Likewise. Can I sit next to you?

Jared nodded, and Eileen got seated in the couch next to Jared. Eileen spoke again:

- So, do tell me. What are you doing here?

Jared:

- Oh, I am sightseeing and enjoying my holiday. I ran into your husband and his friends in Kashmir. It almost cost me my life.

Eileen came closer and whispered softly:

- No, really. What were you doing in Kashmir?

Jared spoke softly:

- I was spying on our old enemies, Pierre Beaumont and Vladimir Kravchenko. Vladimir caught me, ranted about some alien artefacts, and then he knocked me out. When I woke up, I was the captive of two bumbling Indian hitmen. That's when Peng visited me, to reveal that he had paid the hitmen to kill me for being a threat to his marriage.

Eileen:

- My husband wouldn't have travelled all the way to Kashmir for such a small reason, he never cared enough about me to show any kinds of genuine affection.

Jared thought for a second, then spoke:

- Well, he also runs an opium-smuggling operation in that region.

Eileen sighed and replied:

- Then it's true. I saw him meeting with the infamous Mexican drug lord, Jesus Ortega, when we were on a holiday in the Caribbean last year. He denied ever meeting him, but now I know. Peng's financial business must be a front for his drug empire.

Jared:

- You should leave him then.

Eileen:

- Yes. But where will I go? Columnist Party agents will kill me the moment the Emir of Dubai stops protecting me.

Jared:

- I can protect you.

"Eileen, you are not going anywhere!" shrilled a meek and wimpy voice. Eileen and Jared turned to the source of the noise, Eileen's husband Peng was accompanied by two beefed-up bodyguards.
Eileen:

- Peng. What are you doing here?

Peng smirked and replied:

- What kind of husband would I be, if I didn't have access to my wife's private messages so I can prevent her from cheating on me?

Jared:

- Ummm, the respectful and trusting kind?

Peng:

- Don't involve yourself in this, you Aussie scum. I don't know how you escaped India, but escaping Dubai will be even more difficult!

Jared thought about a good reply, but his mind went blank. The only thing he could think about was kissing the beautiful Eileen who sat next to him. As an answer, it wasn't too bad, at least not if she reciprocated his kiss, so Jared gave it a shot. He leaned over, grabbed Eileen and kissed her in front of her jealous and raging husband. For a moment, Eileen forgot all her troubles and she gave out a slight moan of pleasure. Aah!

As expected, Peng didn't appreciate watching another man kissing his wife. Burning with massive anger, Peng's blood pressure shot through the roof and he shouted:

- You shall die for this insult, Jared Pond! Ai-yahh!!

Jared didn't have the time to answer, as Peng's infuriating anger and elevated blood pressure caused the plump Chinese man to have a heart attack, when he was about to ask his guards to capture them both.

Jared turned to the bodyguards and spoke:

- We are leaving. I suggest that you save your boss, he looks like he's about to have a heart attack.

After saying this, Jared grabbed Eileen's hand and they left the coffee shop, while the bodyguards tried to resuscitate Peng.

"SO, WHAT DO WE DO NOW?" Eileen said and smiled as they left the shopping mall.

Jared:

- We are better off leaving Dubai. I doubt the Emir will be happy when he finds out the circumstances around Peng's heart attack.

Eileen:

- But where can we go? Can you protect me in Australia?

Jared reflected over Eileen's question. Bringing Eileen to Australia, which was led by the Columnist Party lapdog Danielle Anders, didn't seem like the best move. But where could they go? If they went to Mexico, they could help the Mexican government deal with Jesus Ortega. In return, the Mexican government could protect them.

Jared:

- No, CPOC operatives have compromised the Australian Government. You wouldn't be safe if you went there.

- However, we could offer our services to the Mexican government. Do you know much about your husband's dealings with Jesus Ortega?

Eileen:

- No, but I grabbed his laptop bag when his bodyguards tried to revive him. With a bit of luck, we can find some useful information on the laptop's hard drive.

Jared:

- Very well. That's our best bet then. Next stop, Mexico City.

After saying this, they grabbed a cab to the airport so they could leave Dubai before the Emir would learn about Peng Jingxing's fate.

Chapter 13: Don't forget about Mexico, 20th January 2040.

Pierre Beaumont was visiting the comatose Martin Orchard in his secret research facility in the Swiss Alps. He wasn't happy with the way things had developed. When Pierre used a replicated Zeto Crystal to bring Martin Orchard back from the dead, he had hoped for a quick recovery. He needed Martin alive and kicking in order to unlock Ben Yehuda's monocle. He also needed Martin to steal the primordial Zeto Crystal from the mysterious Sabina Hines, who had used the crystal's power to become one of the wealthiest and most influential persons in the world.

Pierre was shaking Martin's body, and was about to have a rant, when the chief scientist for the facility, Frank Van Stein, entered the medical room. He approached Pierre, smirked, and spoke:

- Monsieur Beaumont, your medical knowledge must be lacking if you think you can shake a comatose person back to life.

Pierre:

- Don't you dare to make snide remarks. Remember who you are working for.

Frank laughed and replied:

- I know who I am working for, and he looks damn silly shaking a comatose man.

Pierre sighed:

- Hmm. So, what CAN you do to bring back the comatose man in question?

Frank:

- Not much. It's a miracle that he is alive after being dead for years. What did you and Monsieur Kravchenko do to him?

Pierre:

- That's none of your business.

Pierre was interrupted by a phone call from Josefina Fiero. He sighed. Why did his South American associate have to disturb him at such an ill-timed moment? Pierre replied to the phone call:

- Yes, Josefina? What is it?

Josefina:

- Is that how you are greeting your important guest, Pierre? I am at your mansion and your employees don't know where you are.

Hearing this, Pierre recalled agreeing to meet with Josefina about their plans for Mexico and the La Prensa de la Muerte Dam project. The dam was crucial for their plans for their region. Officially, the dam would provide much needed clean hydroelectric power. Pierre's real motive, however, was to submerge prime agricultural lands to create a crop shortage in Mexico. Once the population were starving, it would be easier for Pierre and his accomplices to exert influence in the region.

Pierre:

- Very well. Please enjoy the beverage selection in my lounge room. I will be with you shortly.

HAVING SAID THIS, PIERRE hung up the phone, turned to Frank, and spoke:

- Monsieur Stein. Make sure to bring Mr Orchard to consciousness. Do not fail me, as failure often comes with adverse consequences.

Frank smirked but he didn't reply, and he gave Pierre a long look as Pierre left the lab to meet with Josefina.

JOSEFINA FIERO WAS smoking a cigarette and biting her nails while waiting for Pierre in the lounge room of Palace Beaumont. There had been complications with their plans in Mexico, and Josefina feared for the safety of her adopted daughter Sandra Santiago, who was on an undercover mission. Sandra was participating in the Monocle Conspiracy's scheme to overturn the Mexican government through having an affair with the drug lord Jesus Ortega. Things had turned dangerous when Jared Pond and Eileen Lu had approached the Mexican president, Ana Moreno, with evidence linking Peng Jingxing and Jesus Ortega. The evidence proved that outside forces were at play to overthrow the Mexican government and Josefina feared what would happen if the Mexicans found the connection to Sandra.

Pierre entered the room, coughed, and whinged:

- What kind of behaviour is this? Why are you smoking inside my house? Such 20th century-like behaviour!

Josefina had a fit, threw a glass into the wall, and exclaimed:

- Shut up, Pierre. Because of your incompetence, Sandra is in danger.

Pierre:

- Bah, how can I be responsible for the wellbeing of that spoilt child of yours?

Josefina:

- You and Vladimir captured Jared Pond the Australian spy, and you decided to keep him alive. He escaped and he is now collaborating with Eileen Lu to sell us out to the Mexican president, Ana Moreno.

Pierre reflected over Josefina's rant. It was an interesting twist of fate that Vladimir's desire to keep Jared alive was risking their objectives in Mexico. It was, however, a manageable risk. Pierre opened the file he had on Ana Moreno and he experienced a minor shock. Ana Moreno was the younger sister of the US President-Elect Eva Moreno, whose ambitions had ended with a .50 calibre bullet to her head, in the year 2028.

Pierre:

- I understand your frustration. Since this was Vladimir's mistake, it seems fair that he will need to fix it. I will send him to Mexico to remove Ana Moreno from the presidency, before she can cause us any undue problems.

- Now please let us enjoy some food and drinks. Despite your outburst, you are a valued guest at Palace Beaumont, and you deserve our best hospitality.

Having said this, Pierre rang a bell and a wait staff approached him and Josefina with a selection of exquisite food and drinks. They proceeded to make their plans for Mexico, but during the long discussion, Pierre could only think about one thing. He needed to make sure that Martin Orchard was to be revived. Martin was the only one who could steal the Primordial Zeto Crystal from Sabina Hines, which was the only thing that could bring his true heir, Delphine Beaumont, back to life.

THE FOLLOWING DAY, Pierre met with Vladimir Kravchenko in an upmarket restaurant in Budapest, Hungary. Pierre didn't like the way Vladimir had handled recent events, as it seemed like Vladimir had lost respect for his strategic brilliance. Pierre concluded that Vladimir was making a good call in sidestepping him. After all, only two months had passed since Vladimir saved him from his botched suicide attempt following Delphine's death. Vladimir followed strength, so Pierre needed to show strength to make things go back as they were.

Once they got seated, Vladimir ordered two steaks, extra rare, accompanied by a bottle of Russian vodka. Pierre gave him a disapproving look and spoke:

- Why would I eat barbaric food like that? Raw meat? Russian Vodka? You know me better than that.

Vladimir smirked and replied:

- You do not have to eat or drink anything. I have a mission for you. It is better if you stay sober and hungry.

Pierre gave Vladimir a curious look. 'It has come to this; Vladimir is taking over.' Pierre thought.

Pierre:

- What is the meaning of this? I am the one giving you missions, not the other way around.

Vladimir:

- You have gone too soft. You need to get your hands dirty from time to time. Doing this is the your only way to save Delphine.

Pierre:

- What difference does it make to you?

Vladimir:

- I don't follow weakness. Show strength or I'll take everything from you. Be the man I used to love.

Pierre sighed. He could see Vladimir's point, but how would succumbing to his demands affect their relationship and his future ambitions. Pierre decided to find out more:

- I am curious. What is the mission you have in mind for me?

Vladimir:

- The Romanian arms dealer Roman Ardelean owns a replicated Zeto Crystal. The crystal is weak and insignificant, in comparison to Primordial crystal, but it will be enough to wake Martin Orchard up from his coma. I want you to fetch the crystal for us. An easy task.

Pierre:

- What do I need to do?

Vladimir:

- Enter Roman's mansion, kill the guards and steal the crystal from his safe. Leave no survivors. Easy enough.

Pierre:

- Can't I buy the crystal from him? It's useless to him and I am the wealthiest man in the world.

Vladimir:

- That wouldn't get your hands dirty, would it? Do as I say or face the consequences.

Pierre nodded and didn't argue against Vladimir's demand. Mostly because he didn't want to anger the volatile Russian but also because Vladimir was correct. It was time for him to get his hands dirty. After sitting in silence while watching Vladimir drink and eat the rare steaks, Pierre finally spoke:

- I am ready. I will rise to the occasion. I will be strong so Delphine can have another lease on life.

Vladimir:

- Excellent. Let's go.

After saying this, the men got up and headed for the van where Vladimir had made the plans for the attack.

Chapter 14: The Budapest assault 22nd January 2040.

D ong, Dong, Dong
Pierre Beaumont heard the church bells from the nearby St. Anna's Church strike for midnight. It was time for Pierre to act. Pierre had always preferred to direct missions from the back, but this wouldn't be the first time he encountered action. He had survived the chaos that ensued when the Hei Bai-virus struck New York in 2021 and he had also survived when Zetan Sentry robots had attacked him in Colombia in 2026. This was, however, over a decade earlier.

Pierre was twiddling with the adrenaline shot he held in his hand. His body was frail, and he was unsure if the adrenaline was enough to help him succeed with the mission. However, he had one thing to help him on his quest, his Zetan Monocle, which in combat mode made him the equal of at least 10 elite soldiers.

Pierre toggled the combat mode interface on his monocle, and he programmed it to the parameters of success. To his expectation, the monocle showed him the infrared signature of all the guard in Roman Ardelean's mansion, as well as Roman's position and the location of his vault. At the bottom of the screen, there were two stats. Chance of success: 42 %, Chance of survival: 52 %. Pierre turned off combat mode, turned to Vladimir, and spoke:

- I don't like those odds that the monocle is showing me. There is only a 52 % chance of surviving the mission. I rather not flip a coin about my survival.

Vladimir:

- Hmm. My monocle gives me a 98.5 % chance of survival. Your odds would be much better if you weren't so frail.

Pierre:

- Bah, you know me. I am much more interested in expanding my mind, rather than expanding my muscles.

Vladimir:

- In any case, take the adrenaline shot. It should improve your combat performance.

Pierre followed Vladimir's suggestion, and he injected himself with the adrenaline shot. The adrenaline shot gave Pierre a huge surge of energy, but it also made him worry about his heart arrhythmia. As he entered combat mode again, his chance of survival had increased to 72 %, while his chance of success had fallen to 40 %. This confused Pierre and he turned to Vladimir:

- That's strange. Why has my chance of survival increased but my chance of success fallen?

Vladimir:

- Your monocle shows the odds for a snapshot of time. As time passes, things change, and the odds fluctuates. You should go now before your adrenaline wears off.

Pierre:

- Yes. But before I go, can you promise me one thing? If I die, please resurrect Delphine and rule the world together with my daughter. She is the future of House Beaumont.

Vladimir:

- Ha-ha. If you die you won't know whether I fulfil the promise or not. However, you have my word. It would be my pleasure shaping the future together with Delphine.

Pierre:

- Thank you.

Having said this, Pierre put on a mask and hurried to carry out the mission.

SWOOSH, BANG

Pierre felt an immense rush of adrenaline as he shot the first guard in the garden of Roman's mansion. He dragged the corpse off the path into the bushes, out of sight from the other patrols. Pierre followed the prompts on his monocle, and he snuck past the guard who guarded the main entrance, and he sneaked into the mansion via an open window. This control prompt perplexed him, since he intended to kill all the guards, so what was the point of leaving one alive for now?

Pierre didn't want to second-guess the advanced Zetan technology, so he followed the prompts and entered the bathroom of the palace.

Shclick, poof, bang

Pierre felt a deep sense of gratification that was almost orgasmic, when he shot the second guard with a few bullets through the toilet door. Two down, six to go. The control prompt on Pierre's monocle told him to keep walking down the great hall and climb a set of stairs. When Pierre reached the set of stairs, he was distracted by a half-open wardrobe, with the glimpse of a naked body. Following his morbid curiosity, he opened the wardrobe and he let out a loud shriek when he saw a mutilated female body hanging from a rope.

Danger, enemy approaching flashed on Pierre's screen. Pierre turned around, but it was too late, and he flinched from pain and dropped his gun when a bullet hit him in the arm. Injured and unarmed, Pierre didn't stand a chance when Roman's henchman ran up to him and knocked him out.

"PIERRE BEAUMONT. I would never expect us to meet like this."

Pierre opened his eyes and he was tied up to a chair in Roman's office in the mansion. Roman, who was dressed in a red velvet suit, smiled towards Pierre with his golden teeth and wicked grin. Roman spoke again:

- Why are you here? You must understand my amazement. In my line of work, assassination attempts are common, but I never expected the CEO of the World Bank to come himself.

- What could possibly be your motive?

Pierre paused and consulted his monocle. 'Telling the truth is the most favourable outcome.' The Monocle displayed. Pierre replied:

- I came here to kill you and steal one of your possessions. I want the blue crystal that you store in your safe.

After hearing this, Roman walked to his safe, entered the passkey, took out the replicated Zeto Crystal, showed it to Pierre, and spoke:

- Do you mean this crystal? What value does it have to the richest man in the world?

Pierre:

- There are things about me that you don't know, and which you don't need to know. All you need to know is that I am willing to pay you $10 million for the crystal and a safe passage from your mansion, if you let me go.

Hearing this, Roman walked up to Pierre, punched him in the face, and exclaimed:

- You greedy pig. You are insulting me. You planned to murder me, you killed two of my men, and now you're trying to pay me off? Fuck you, Pierre.

Pierre:

- Should I interpret that as you being uncooperative?

Roman:

- Damn right!

Pierre:

- That's unfortunate, then I will have to kill you.

Hearing Pierre's threat, Roman punched him in the face, and taunted:

- Don't make me laugh.

Pierre:

- Trust me, I will have the last laugh.

After saying this, Pierre contacted Vladimir via the monocle. A few seconds later, there was a loud noise of shattered window glass as Vladimir, attached to an abseiling rope, leapt through the broken window straight into the room. As he landed, Vladimir disconnected the rope and pulled his semi-automatic pistols from his holsters. It was all over in a matter of seconds, as the security guards lay dead on the floor and Roman collapsed in agony with bullets to his kneecaps.

Pierre looked at Roman and spoke:

- You should have taken my offer, Roman.

After Vladimir loosened Pierre's tied hands, he stomped Roman's head several times, until brain matter splashed on his shoes.

Vladimir smiled and looked at Pierre:

- Not exactly a clean crime scene, there will be so much cleaning up to do. Did you find the replicated Zeto Crystal?

Pierre:

- Yes, I got it.

Vladimir:

- Good. Let's burn down the place and leave. You failed the challenge as you didn't leave a clean crime scene. *wink*

Pierre:

- I didn't fail. Everyone is dead and we got the crystal.

Vladimir:

- Yes, thanks to me. Never mind, it was a pleasure watching you in the field. It's an exhilarating feeling when you're killing people up close and personal, isn't it?

Pierre:

- Yes, I haven't felt this alive for years.

Vladimir:

- I don't doubt that at all. Speaking of which, it's time to go back and revive that son of a gun Martin Orchard. He'll steal the Primordial Zeto Crystal from Sabina for us and victory will be ours.

Pierre nodded and smiled. Vladimir had done the right thing by forcing him to take part in the killing. He felt more energised than he had felt in years and he couldn't wait to see how the rest of his plans would play out. After initiating a fire to destroy evidence by burning the entire building, Pierre and Vladimir left Roman's mansion as quickly as they could.

Chapter 15: A meeting with the Mexican president, 1st February 2040

Jared Pond and Eileen Lu were sitting in the garden of the presidential palace in Mexico City. It was a lush tropical garden, full of exotic birds and animals. If it wasn't for the many military checkpoints on the way to the palace, Mexico would seem like a paradise. However, they knew better. Mexico was a country on the brink of civil war.

Eileen and Jared were drinking horchatas (a thick rice and almond drink) in the shade when President Ana Moreno approached them. Ana spoke:

- Welcome to the presidential residence. As I understand it, you have provided our federal police with important evidence linking the criminal Jesus Ortega with Peng Jingxing, who in turn relates to some very powerful people.

Eileen:

- Yes. Evidence on Peng's computer showed large amount of bank transfers to Mexican charities where Jesus Ortega's group is the beneficiary. Among their greatest sponsors are the World Bank, the Emir of Dubai, and a Brazilian business tycoon Josefina Fiero.

Ana:

- I know about this situation. What I don't know is whether I can trust the two of you. Eileen, you are legally married to Peng, and instead of accompanying him in the hospital after his heart attack, you chose to run away with your former lover, Jared Pond. I am sorry, but that doesn't improve your credibility.

Eileen:

- I know what it looks like, but hear me out. The Emir offered me political asylum and forced me to marry Peng after the Chinese Columnist Party staged a coup against me. I accepted my fate, but I truly believed that Peng was nothing but a legitimate businessman. After finding out that he was involved in drug smuggling in Mexico and was in fact supporting terrorism, I couldn't stay with him any longer.

Ana:

- You're making some good points, but I am still not convinced.

Eileen:

- President Moreno, please listen. You've got to believe me. Now that I have lost the Emir's protection, Chinese Columnist Party agents will come after me. The only way for the two of us to survive is to cooperate. I knew your sister Eva Moreno well, when I was the president of China. We tried to make the world a better place through uncovering the dark elements hiding in the shadows. The conspiracy we are up against murdered your sister and forced me into exile and a forced marriage. We can set things straight if you believe me.

Being reminded of her sister's murder, Ana shivered, and a few tears ran down her cheeks. She poured herself a glass of water, drank it, and spoke:

- I never believed in the official narrative regarding my sister's death. Why would the then vice president, Jonathan Feng, collaborate with the Chinese and Iranian governments to have her murdered? It didn't make any sense. However, I had to move on, and I hope Eva's spirit can live on through me and my actions.

Jared Pond, who had been silent during the whole conversation, joined in:

- I believe that the Monocle Conspiracy was behind both the release of the deadly Hei Bai virus and the assassination of your sister. At the centre of the conspiracy, stands the evil mastermind Pierre Beaumont. Other notable members are the CIA director James Winter, the former US president Damien Vanderbilt, and Pierre's attack dog Vladimir Kravchenko.

Ana:

- Do you have any evidence for these claims?

Jared:

- If I did, I wouldn't be a washed-up agent, while evil men like Pierre rule the world.

Ana:

- I understand. This must be related to the La Prensa de la Muerte dam that Pierre wants to build in Mexico. There has been non-stop propaganda about the importance of building the dam to Mexican citizens wealth and prosperity. I believe doing so would actually diminish our prime agricultural lands and starve our people.

Eileen:

- If one repeats a lie enough times, it becomes the truth.

Ana:

- Yes, that's why I need you to do something for me. I need you to gather intel on Jesus Ortega and his group. My government agencies are compromised, but perhaps you can find out the truth.

Eileen:

- I would be honoured to help you, Ana. We need to find those responsible for Eva's death and stop Mexico from descending into chaos.

Ana:

- Thank you. I must leave now. My aides will provide you with all the assistance the presidential office can offer you.

After saying this, Ana walked away. Eileen studied the president intently. She resembled the late Eva Moreno, but she seemed more pragmatic and less idealistic in comparison to her. Perhaps that was a good thing. Eileen had a lot of great ideas but no means of implementing them during her years as China's president. Would things had been different if she had focused on strengthening her power before she tried to change things?

Eileen brushed off her thoughts. There was nothing she could do about her past, and the future was all that mattered. Whatever Pierre had planned for Mexico, she owed the Mexican population and the rest of the world to stop him. She turned to Jared and spoke:

- Let's head back to our hotel, hun. I am feeling a little tired.

Jared:

- What about seeking help from President Moreno's operatives? We should perhaps ask some of the intelligence officers before getting back to the hotel.

Eileen:

- You heard how she mentioned that our enemy has infiltrated her government? If we want to achieve our goal, we are better off acting without external assistance.

Jared:

- Very well. Let's leave this place.

After saying this, they finished their horchatas and they left the palace without seeking government help.

EILEEN STUDIED THE naked body of her lover Jared, who slept next to her in a muggy rundown hostel. The sex wasn't as good as she remembered it. Were her memories wrong, or was it simply the effect of aging? Eileen studied Jared's scars. They gave him character, and also reminded her about the past they shared. Jared had a lot of scars on his body, many of them had been caused by Chairman Jing Xi's thugs in 2021, before they escaped from Columnist Party captivity.

A cockroach crawled up on Eileen's arm, and she held back a scream of disgust while brushing it away. She didn't want to wake Jared up, and besides, she would have to settle for places like this for the time being. There weren't many hotels that accepted cash payments without any form of identification, and they needed to stay off the grid.

Eileen looked at her phone. A tiny part of her wanted to turn the phone on and contact her husband to tell him that she has regretted what she had done. If she could reconcile with her husband, she could resume her rich and easy life as a bored housewife, living in wealth and luxury. Eileen brushed off the idea. It was more likely that her husband would send someone to kill her than take her back, and even if he did forgive her, what life would it become. Did she want to spend the rest of her life in a gilded cage, being the property of her drug-smuggling and terrorism-financing fat husband?

Eileen kissed Jared's ear gently. She was right where fate intended her to be. If she could make the world a better place by stopping Pierre's evil schemes, it was her obligation to do so. If she were to fail, they could take her life, but they could never again take her freedom.

Chapter 16: Welcome back, Mr Orchard, 8th February 2040

Vladimir Kravchenko was testing a nerve-pain-amplifier on some unwilling test subjects in the Beaumont Science Centre in the Swiss Alps. Finding willing test subjects for the nerve-pain-amplifier was out of the question, as the pain this device could create was unbearable. However, Vladimir had found a workaround to this issue. He had recruited human traffickers to provide him with an infinite supply of refugees for his cruel human experiments. Thus, the people that ended up being Vladimir's lab rats inadvertently spent their life savings thinking they could get better lives, to receive an excruciatingly painful death instead. Vladimir couldn't stop himself from smiling wickedly when he thought about this cruel but humorous irony of fate.

"Monsieur Kravchenko. I have some great news. One of our test subjects survived all our pain enduring tests."

Vladimir turned around and looked at Chief Scientist Frank Van Stein. Vladimir smiled and spoke:

- Excellent. Can you take me to this test subject at once?

Frank nodded and he led Vladimir to another room, where five out of the six test subjects had died. He turned to Frank and spoke:

- Hmm, this is an interesting development. I thought everyone in this room had the same setting on their nerve-pain-amplifiers. Why did this one survive, when the others died?

Frank:

- I had a dream last night. In my vision, Akram had his nerve-pain-amplifiers set to setting 5B. I needed to find out if it works, so I changed his setting.

Vladimir:

- Setting the pain level to 5B? Wasn't that the worst setting in the past? Everyone died within minutes.

Frank:

- Yes. But somehow it seems to work better with our new prototype of nanotechnology drones.

Vladimir:

- Interesting. I will go through another cycle with the surviving test subject. If your assumption is correct, he should survive the new process too.

Having said this, Vladimir walked up to Akram, who looked exhausted, drenched in cold sweat and with blood running from his nose. Vladimir spoke:

- Akram Hazaryan. Welcome to the Beaumont Science Centre. I am Vladimir Kravchenko, and I am the co-owner of this facility.

Akram:

- What have I done to you? Why are you torturing me? Why did you murder my family?

Vladimir:

- I can assure you, Mr Hazaryan, that this has do nothing to do with you or your family. Destiny has simply put you in the way of my marvellous creation.

Vladimir flipped a switch, and a hologram showed up next to them. The hologram showcased a schematic of the nerve-pain-amplifying nanorobots. Vladimir:

- Behold the new nerve-pain-amplifier. With this device, I can afflict any form of pain to you through pressing a button on my smartphone. We have been developing this device for years, but you are the only survivor we have had this far.

Akram cringed and said:

- But why do you need this technology to torture us? What have we done to you?

Vladimir:

- You need to see the big picture. With this device, I can control people from afar. Not everyone fears dying, but everyone fears indefinite suffering.

Akram:

- What are you going to do to me, you wicked monster?!

Vladimir:

- I want to gain absolute control over humanity. My associate, Pierre Beaumont, has strived to control humanity through his power, money, and the media for the last decades. But it's ineffective and you'll always find dissent. I aim to develop the nerve-pain-amplifier and spread it across the globe using Pierre's money and influence. Once everyone has the nerve-pain-amplifier installed, I'll be in complete control of their pain response. Once I control people's pain, I'll control their behaviour.

- But enough of the wishy-washy talk. I got to run another test to see if the device is working.

Having said this, Vladimir activated the device and pressed the 'Full body On Fire' button. It was one of the most dangerous settings that killed most of the test subjects, but he needed to find out if Frank had told him the truth. Vladimir studied Akram, who was rolling around on the floor in agonizing pain. Could Akram survive three minutes of this torture?

As three minutes had passed, Vladimir turned off the device, and he watched how Akram got back to his senses. Akram whispered and said:

- Please make it stop. I'll do anything for you.

Vladimir:

- I did make it stop. Now enjoy your sensation of brain haemorrhage.

Having said this, Vladimir set the device to give Akram a sensation of his brain haemorrhaging. He left his test subject writhing in pain, approached Frank, and spoke:

- Very well, Dr Stein. It seems like you have found the solution to our
  little problem. Give me a set of the implants that Akram has. I have
  a very special test subject for our next trial.

As Frank handed him the nanotechnology chips, Vladimir shone with glee. It was time for the bastard Martin Orchard to pay the price for his betrayal in Jerusalem.

"FRANK TOLD ME YOU FINALLY got the nerve-pain amplifier to work," Pierre said and smiled while he was slurping some oysters with beluga caviar for lunch.

Vladimir studied Pierre. At some point he would need to double-cross his partner and implant him with the amplifier for his plan to work, but now was not the time. Vladimir spoke cynically:

- Yes. How is the situation with Martin Orchard?

Pierre responded:

- He is slowly recovering, passing in and out of consciousness. I haven't spoken to him about our objectives for him to steal the primordial Zeto Crystal yet.

Vladimir:

- I want to use the nerve-pain-amplifier on Martin. We need to get complete control of him and punish him for his betrayal in the past.

Pierre gave Vladimir a slow look and replied:

- Hmm, you only had a single survivor from the group. I would rather not kill Martin again because of your experiments. It's too much hassle to bring him back to life again.

Vladimir:

- I will do more experiments on the technology once I have secured more test subjects. However, we cannot set Martin free and task him with stealing the primordial Zeto Crystal from Sabina Hines without complete control over him. He will betray us, and if they join forces, they can destroy us.

Pierre sighed and replied:

- You are correct. Let's do things your way.

Vladimir:

- With pleasure. It is time for Martin to pay for his duplicity.

VLADIMIR AND PIERRE entered a secret medical facility which was located under a luxurious resort near Lake Geneva. Pierre had used the resort to butter up greedy world leaders with luxuries such as expensive cruises, recreational drugs, and high-class prostitutes to collect dirt on his political friends and opponents. This was to make sure they complied with his wishes. Vladimir had greater plans for the resort, plans that he hadn't revealed to Pierre yet. Vladimir intended to use the resort as his staging ground for spreading the nerve-pain-amplifiers. Once he had the big wigs implanted with the nerve-pain-amplifiers, he would force them to spread the technology to the rest of the population. Then he would be in complete control of the world, and humanity would tremble at his power.

Vladimir snapped out of his daydreaming when he arrived at Martin's room. His Swedish former co-conspirator looked awful and weak when he was lying unconscious in the nursing bed. Vladimir had expected this. Although Vladimir and Martin were both in their early fifties, Vladimir had the advantage of not being dead and cryogenically frozen for two years.

Vladimir opened Martin's mouth forcefully and made him swallow a microchip with the nerve-pain technology. This was a less effective method than surgically implanting it into his skull, however, Vladimir wanted to avoid Martin from finding out about the microchip as it would give him a surgical scar on his head.

Vladimir smiled when the microchip came online. This meant that it had managed to attach itself to a nerve cell to operate on bioelectricity. "Let's wake him up," Vladimir exclaimed and sent a command to the nerve-pain-amplifier to give Martin a tingling sensation in his body.

Martin woke up with a shock, and Vladimir spoke:

- Welcome back, Mr Orchard.

Martin mumbled:

- What happened? What year is it? I remember that I died in Israel. Why did you revive me, Vladimir?

Pierre interjected:

- All very valid questions, Martin. As for your death, I had hoped you'd remember what caused it. Szymon Yehuda killed you for what you did to his brother Ben Yehuda. You betrayed us, Martin.

Martin sighed:

- So, why did you revive me then?

Pierre:

- We need your help. You will be the person to initiate the transfer of the late Ben Yehuda's monocle to a new owner.

Martin:

- Is that all? Did you bring me back from the dead to fix one of the damaged Zetan monocles?

Pierre:

- Not exactly. We have a more important task for you. You need to retrieve the primordial Zeto Crystal from Sabina Hines. We saw your background history, we now know that she is your biological daughter, so you must help us in retrieving the crystal from her.

Martin:

- What if I don't want to help you? What if I am pissed off that you disturbed my peaceful death?

Vladimir:

- Don't you dare to argue with us after all the hassle I had bringing you back from the dead.

Having said this, Vladimir activated Martin's nerve-pain-amplifier, and Martin screamed in excruciating pain, as if he was on fire. Eventually, Vladimir turned off the amplifier. Martin took a deep breath of relief, and Pierre spoke:

- We have been developing new technology in the last two years. Behold the nerve-pain-amplifier. It can cause you immeasurable pain through manipulating your nerve cells with pain sensory input. The best part is that the device won't kill you, so you'll face endless torture if you decide to oppose us.

Martin:

- What if I rather kill myself to fuck the two of you off?

Vladimir:

- Then we'll resurrect you. I have a specific torture chamber at the Beaumont Science Centre dedicated just for you.

Martin:

- Fucking hell, the two of you are real assholes. Okay, I'll submit to your demands. What do you need?

Pierre:

- Like I said, first you must unlock Ben Yehuda's monocle. As for the rest of the mission I am happy to discuss it over dinner upstairs. We are in the basement of the finest hospitality venue in the world after all.

After saying this, Pierre snapped his fingers and Jean Valmont brought a tailor-made suit for Martin and left.
Pierre:

- Don't just lie there, Martin. Get dressed. It's time to get some food.

The Swede got up from the bed and got dressed, feeling amazed that his pains had receded as quickly as they came. After that, the trio walked to the lift to enjoy some fine dining.

"I DON'T TRUST HIM. I want to follow him along the way and see what he is up to." Vladimir said as he and Pierre had a private rendezvous. Pierre smirked and replied:

- Of course, you don't. He is unreliable and bound to betray us. But he did unlock Ben Yehuda's monocle, and he will lead us to Sabina Hines and the Primordial Zeto Crystal. Once he does, we paralyse him from afar, and move in with our troops and secure the Crystal.

Vladimir:

- So, was this all a plan to deceive him?

Pierre:

- Yes, he hates us, and he will be more inclined to help his daughter. We should use this to our advantage. Take a group of your finest mercenaries. Keep him under surveillance but stay out of his way. We will know when it is time to strike.

Vladimir:

- Yes, Pierre. I will do your bidding.

Pierre:

- Excellent. I saw that he booked a flight to Copenhagen. Follow him there and see what he is up to. Dismissed.

Vladimir:

- So, you are not up for cuddles tonight?

Pierre:

- We can "cuddle" once the primordial Zeto Crystal is in our hands and both Martin Orchard and Sabina Hines are resting in their graves. Now go, my humble servant. Time is of the essence and we cannot allow Martin to disappear on us.

Vladimir nodded and left the room to assemble his team of lethal mercenaries to keep Martin under surveillance.

Chapter 17: "Who is that girl, Martin?" 5th March 2040.

P ierre Beaumont was sitting in one of the World Bank's offices in Sydney, Australia. He was having a meeting with his obedient Australian lapdog, Prime Minister Danielle Anders. He needed to investigate why Danielle had sent Jared Pond after him. There was, however, another detail that bothered him more than the ungrateful transgender Australian PM, he couldn't figure out who Martin Orchard's latest accomplice was.

Vladimir's men had taken photographs of the mysterious girl and she had matched the identity of a certain Sara Nilsson from Sweden. Pierre had suspected that something was amiss, and he had sent his men to question Sara Nilsson's parents in Sweden. They had confirmed his suspicions. Sara Nilsson had died a few years earlier, and whoever Martin was working with had assumed a false identity. Since it was extremely difficult to hack the global passport database in the year 2040, this meant that Sara was one of the best hackers in the world.

Pierre got distracted when the receptionist called him:

- Mr Beaumont. Prime Minister Danielle Anders is here to see you.

Pierre:

- Very well, send her in.

Pierre felt irritated when the ugly transvestite Danielle entered his office wearing an extremely thick facemask. Danielle who used to been known as Daniel, was the Columnist Party puppet premier of Victoria, just a few decades earlier. Unsurprisingly, after two decades of aging and her gender change, things hadn't improved, particularly not her looks.

When deciding to support Danielle's ambitions to become the Australian PM, Pierre had been trolling the Australian public. He had never anticipated that he could make a PM out of the man who escaped Australia after his ties to the Columnist Party became public. In any case, Danielle was now the PM of Australia and Pierre had to deal with her.

Pierre:

- Take off that bloody mask, Danielle. I want to see your face. Why are you wearing a disguise anyway?

Danielle spoke in a pretentious and unpleasant high pitch:

- Mr Beaumont. Your secretary told me that we needed to discuss the repercussions of the spread of Norovirus-40B to the general public. As per your instruction, I have asked media to spread terrible death scenarios to terrify the public of this mild virus.

Pierre sighed. He was getting old and it became more and more difficult keeping track of the lies he told the ignorant masses. Pierre said:

- Cancel it. I am sick of looking at people wearing masks and media fearmongering.

Danielle:

- Cancel the spread of the virus?

Pierre:

- Yes. Stop testing everyone and stop reporting about it. It was fun seeing so much mayhem and chaos escalated from unknowing fools. I no longer want to use a viral disease to scare the Australian public.

Danielle:

- Understood. So, what are we going to fearmonger about this year?

Pierre:

- I don't know. I will get back to you about that, when I feel like it.

Danielle:

- So, what is the purpose of our meeting then?

Pierre:

- You know why you are here. I helped you rise to power and you repaid my kindness by sending Jared Pond to spy on me. I want you to send your operatives to kill him. This is your mess, so you better fix it. You also need to support Jesus Ortega against President Ana Moreno in Mexico. We need that dam built in Mexico, to have power over the region.

Danielle:

- Understood. How can I help Jesus Ortega to usurp power?

Pierre:

- Send your best assassins to Mexico. After they've dealt with Jared, they can help Jesus assassinate Ana.

Danielle:

- Understood, Mr Beaumont. My sincere apologies for breaking your trust.

Pierre:

- Whatever. Get your unpleasant face out of here, I will summon you if the need arises.

Danielle held back her anger. Pierre should tread lightly. While he was the most powerful man in the world, Australia was her country, and he shouldn't dare to insult her looks. Danielle reminded herself that Vladimir Kravchenko was in Sydney, accompanied by a group of mercenaries. If she were to confront Pierre, she would no doubt lose her head. Keeping this in mind, Danielle put on her facemask, bowed to Pierre, and hurried to leave the office.

"WHO IS THAT GIRL, MARTIN? Remember that your mission to Australia is to steal the primordial Zeto Crystal from Sabina Hines." Pierre muttered as he met his Swedish co-conspirator in a restaurant in Barangaroo. Martin gave him a sceptical look and replied:

- Her name is Sara Nilsson. I decided to hire someone of similar age as Sabina to help me find out more about her. We are interviewing people surrounding Sabina to find out where she might hide the Zeto Crystal.

Pierre:

- Bah. Sara Nilsson is an assumed identity. My men cross-examined Sara Nilsson's parents in Sweden. She has been dead since November 2037.

Martin:

- Alas, I don't have the luxury and resources to do comprehensive background checks on my employees. Sara is a very talented researcher and crucial in helping me find avenues into convincing Sabina to give up the primordial Zeto Crystal to us.

Pierre:

- Bah, I don't believe a word you are saying. I give you until the end of the month. If you haven't given me the primordial Zeto Crystal by then, I will send Vladimir to take it forcefully from your daughter. That won't be pretty. Do we have an understanding?

Martin:

- Yes, Pierre. I understand you.

Pierre:

- Good. As for you, please enjoy the preview of what your life will entail if you fail me.

Having said this, Pierre sent a signal to Martin's nerve-pain-amplifier to emulate the pain of a few broken bones. As Martin collapsed to the floor, screaming in agony, Pierre smirked, left a few hundred dollars for the bill, and exited the restaurant.

"I NEED YOU TO GET MORE mercenaries." Pierre said to Vladimir as they were sharing a bottle of wine in the spa of an upmarket brothel. Vladimir gave him a curious look, sculled the wine, and replied:

- Why? I have an expert group with me, perfectly capable of dealing with the threat that Martin and Sabina pose. We have concluded that Sabina has no armed men working for her.

Pierre followed Vladimir's example and poured himself a glass of wine, took Vladimir's hand, looked him in the eyes, and spoke:

- I suspect that others might want to get involved. I had a confrontation with Danielle Anders earlier today. We need to make sure that she always has men following her, to prevent her from getting any disobedient ideas. But I am more worried about Elaine Orchard. She has the wealth to stand up to us and she controls the Harapan Conglomerate, the largest entity in South East Asia. She might want to get involved to save Martin and steal the Zeto Crystal for herself.

Vladimir digested Pierre's words. He didn't agree with his financier and mentor. Pierre was getting out of touch with reality. Engaging more mercenaries didn't do anything to promote their chance of success, quite the opposite. If they hired too many, it would be impossible to keep a tight ship and word would get out that they were up to something. This would attract the attention of other groups that also sought the primordial Zeto Crystal. Since Sabina Hines had unearthed the primordial Zeto Crystal two years earlier, the different factions in the Monocle Conspiracy had been watching each other waiting for someone to make the first move. If Pierre hired more mercenaries, they would attract the attention of the Yehuda's Mossad, James Winter's CIA operatives, the Indonesian Harapan Conglomerate led by Elaine Orchard, and the Avanço Verde-Ouro Corporation by Josefina Fiero. It was impossible to predict who would come out of this scenario alive.

Vladimir snapped out of it. Apart from his far-fetched dream of controlling the planet with the nerve-pain-amplifier, the scenario of an all-out battle in Sydney for the control of the Primordial Zeto Crystal also appealed to him. The greatest moment of Vladimir's life was when he freed Eileen and Jared from the Chinese Columnist Party's captivity back in 2021. He had levelled entire blocks in the carnage, and if he could experience that orgasmic chaos again, it was worth the risk of losing everything. Vladimir poured himself yet another glass and spoke:

> - Okay, Pierre. I will get us more mercenaries. As for now, get us a large selection of young fresh male and female dominatrices. I am starving and this should be an orgy to remember!

After watching Pierre put through the order, Vladimir held him down and took him from behind forcefully, while Pierre moaned in exhilaration and pleasure. The thoughts of all the deaths to come made Vladimir insanely aroused, and this would be an orgy to remember.

Chapter 18: "We got to help Martin ASAP, Budi." 15th March 2040

The chief of Security for the Harapan Conglomerate, Budi Sepulyat, was checking out pro-terrorism photos online when Elaine Orchard entered his office. He panicked and turned off the screen, but realised that it was too late when Elaine spoke:

- So, this is how you are keeping us safe? It's a miracle that any of us are alive!

Budi:

- I am sorry, Ratu (Queen) Elaine. It won't happen again.

Elaine:

- In any case, I didn't come here to lecture you about your religious habits.

- Something is up. We got to help Martin ASAP, Budi.

Budi gave Elaine a confused look. He could swear that she had been very upset a few years earlier when Martin had been shot dead on a mission in Jerusalem. While Elaine never gave him the exact details of what happened to Martin, he was certain that Martin died. Budi said:

- I am sorry, Ratu Elaine. I feel so stupid, but isn't Martin already dead?

Elaine:

- Don't feel stupid. He did die. However, I found out that Pierre brought him back from the dead. Pierre and Vladimir have implanted Martin with a device that gives him insufferable pain if he doesn't do their bidding. They are moving in on the primordial Zeto Crystal. We need to stop them, save Martin, and steal the primordial Zeto Crystal for ourselves.

Budi:

- Understood, my queen. What do you need me to do?

Elaine:

- Bring your men to the presentation level. We are meeting our Chief Scientist Rexi Lembong in one hour. We'll present the plan for you then.

Budi:

- Understood, Ratu Elaine.

Elaine:

- Good.

- Oh, and don't let me distract you from your sick and twisted "religious dogmas".

Having said this, Elaine left the office while Budi was stuck with red cheeks from embarrassment, trying to figure out what to do about his "religious dogmas".

BUDI SEPULYAT MADE his way to the presentation level an hour later. Most of his men were already there, while Elaine and Rexi seemed to be debating over the structure of a 3D hologram building. Budi cleared his throat to alert Elaine of his presence:

- Security Chief Budi Sepulyat, reporting for duty.

Elaine:

- Tsk, tsk, tsk. Did I tell you to spend that much time with your personal hobbies?

Budi's cheeks turned red and Elaine spoke again:

- Don't worry about it. What matters is the mission at hand. Rexi, can you fill Budi in?

Rexi got up, stretched and corrected his posture. He spoke to the gathered group:

- We have a very difficult and dangerous task ahead of us. Vladimir Kravchenko and his group of mercenaries are in Sydney. They aim to murder Martin Orchard and steal a priceless alien artefact. It is our job to stop them. Our main concern is Vladimir Kravchenko who is equipped with alien technology that makes him the most dangerous warrior to ever walk the Earth.

Elaine added in:

- Don't fear. A single woman defeated Vladimir in 2028, and you are the best fighting group Indonesia has ever seen. You'll prevail.

The group chanted:

- Kami akan menang. Hidup Indonesia dan Konglomerat Harapan. (We shall prevail. Long live Indonesia and the Harapan Conglomerate)

After a while, Elaine raised her hand to silence the group, and Rexi spoke again.

- To defeat Vladimir's bloodthirsty devils, we will need discipline. You'll all be wearing Zetan invisibility suits to avoid detection. You'll also wear a suit that cools you down to ambient temperature to avoid detection via the infrared spectrum.

Elaine:

- Thank you, Rexi. You'll join Budi and his men on the mission.

Rexi gave Elaine a strange look and objected:

- But I am your chief scientist. What use can I be on this dangerous mission?

Elaine:

- You need to see how your inventions work in real life. That is the only way you can develop real-world applications. Besides, the group needs your brain as an addition to their brawl.

Rexi sighed and said:

- Understood, Ratu Elaine.

Elaine smiled and replied:

- My fellow men, let's have a feast. Today we celebrate, and tomorrow we go to war.

Having said this, Elaine clapped her hands. On this signal, a group of servants and concubines entered the room to fulfil the men's every desire.

ELAINE ORCHARD WAS watching the skyline from her penthouse in the Harapan Conglomerate Headquarters. She had left the feast early, but to no avail, as she could not sleep. She would soon be at the point beyond return. If she were to fight against Pierre and Vladimir, she would lose her benefactors and make herself some truly dangerous enemies. But what choice did she have? Her spies had told her that Vladimir and Pierre were developing a terrifying torture device that they could implant into people's heads, to control their pain from a distance. If Pierre and Vladimir could spread this technology, they would rule the world with terror. It would be even worse if they found a way to amass the almost limitless energy from the primordial Zeto Crystal. At first, Elaine had doubted her spy reports, but after seeing the CCTV footage of Martin collapsing in agony at a restaurant, she knew they were true. Pierre and Vladimir had implanted Martin with this terrible device to force him to do their bidding.

Elaine took a deep breath, and drank some warm mildly sedating tea. Under the influence of the sedatives, she felt at peace. She needed to stop Pierre and Vladimir. It was her purpose in life to stop them and build the paradise she envisioned. If she were to die trying to build that paradise, it was better than being alive in a dystopian future where Pierre and Vladimir ruled through terror and fear. Having made peace with the risk of dying in the war to come, Elaine leaned back into her bed and fell asleep.

Chapter 19: The Banker meets the Empath, 30th March 2040.

Pierre Beaumont was setting up a market manipulation scheme that would cause chaos on the ASX and make him a few hundred million dollars richer. Although Pierre's wealth was already in the trillions and he had no need to manipulate the markets, it was a pastime that never got old to him.

Pierre picked a few companies to short on the trading market and he risked a billion dollars in each company. The shorts would need to be repaid on Monday, and by then the shares would have plummeted and Pierre could close the shorts and make a fortune. Pierre sent out negative fake news articles about the companies he had shorted, and he would make his media empire push the negative news to bring the share value down. That would fool the unknowing sheep so he could fleece them for even more money.

Pierre checked his share trading account and he smiled when he saw how the share price of the companies he shorted had plummeted, due to his huge amount of propaganda to deliberate create fake news via social media. He was up $100 million from pressing a few buttons, from pushing his lies and debaucheries. Life was glorious on the top.

Pierre checked the list of dignitaries that he was meeting for lunch at the World Economic Forum. He hoped it would be someone interesting. At least the $100,000 he charged for a consultancy meeting would stop the rabble from accessing his valuable time. Pierre's jaw dropped when he noticed who had paid to meet him. Today's lunch meeting would be with Sabina Hines, the mysterious woman who had stolen the primordial Zeto Crystal from Ben Yehuda. But why had Sabina come to see him? The meeting request stated that Sabina needed funding for an ocean clean-up project, and needed to meet Pierre to get a sponsorship agreement. But Sabina was an incredibly successful trader who had made billions of dollars from online trading. She did not need to petition him for charity.

Bouts of paranoia struck Pierre. What if Sabina knew that he was coming after her and had decided to strike first? If that were the case, he needed Vladimir and the mercenaries to protect him, as he feared that his official bodyguards would not be enough against someone with Sabina's abilities. Pierre shook off the idea. He could not bring Vladimir and his armed mercenaries to the World Economic Forum. Bringing armed men to the International Convention Centre in central Sydney would cause too much attention. It would look obscene for him to pose with his private army, and besides, he didn't want the world to know that he did command a private army.

Pierre decided to meet with Sabina without revealing his plans against her. If she had come to snoop on him, he was better off if he knew about the official reason for her visit. Pierre opened the attached document to the meeting request. The proposed automated robot-technology for cleaning up the pollution of the oceans sounded impressive, but he couldn't see how it would benefit his goals, so he would give it a pass. After reading up on Sabina's proposed technology, he ordered coffee and watched his share portfolio, while waiting for Sabina to arrive.

"WARNING. THERE IS A powerful creature in front of you. Proceed with caution."

Pierre studied the message that popped up on his Zetan Monocle, as Sabina entered the meeting room. He had met countless world leaders in the last few decades, but he had never seen this warning before. He studied Sabina. She looked young, beautiful, and harmless. She had a tall and slender physique, and she wasn't carrying any weapons. Pierre doubted that she was a powerful fighter. Even if his bodyguards weren't around, he assumed that he could beat her in a fistfight if he activated combat mode on his monocle, despite his old age.

Pierre's eyes turned to Sabina's husband, Alex. He was also in his early 20's, and he was athletic and extremely handsome. 'Hmm, at least she has a good taste in men.' Pierre thought and reflected whether Alex was his key to forcing Sabina to submit to his will. Pierre turned to Sabina and spoke:

- As you know, my time is valuable, but I will give you ten minutes to make your case as for why the World Bank should assist you.

Pierre felt surprised when Alex started talking about their proposal and this annoyed him. Pierre knew that it was Sabina who had stolen the Zeto Crystal and made billions of dollars from using its supernatural powers. To send her husband who was nothing but a pretty face of her organisation to do the talking, was downright insulting and Pierre wondered why Sabina didn't speak herself. After listening to Alex's presentation, Pierre replied:

- Yes, I have heard about your utopian project and the bank's final answer is a NO.

Alex pleaded:

- But why, it could save a lot of marine life at a low cost.

Pierre:

- We do not prioritise marine life, and the World Bank has a lot of missions on its hands.

For the first time, Sabina opened her mouth and replied:

- Geez. We paid $100,000 to meet you. At least you can give us a proper answer.

'Oh, she is a fiery one,' Pierre thought and smiled. He got back to his cold personality and replied:

- While cleaning up the oceans is a worthwhile goal, the ocean is owned by everyone and it is nothing the bank can invest in. The bank does not deal with utilitarian means. We deal with assets.

Sabina:

- What about creating a better world?

Pierre:

- Everything good has a monetary value; clean oceans do not. Thus, it is not for us to pursue.

Hearing Pierre's arrogant and condescending tone, Sabina lashed out:

- Money is not everything in the world.

Pierre smirked and replied:

- That is where the bank must disagree with you. Money does not exist to serve humans. Humans exist to serve money. In the absence of deities, money becomes the new god, the raison d'être for humanity.

Pierre smirked at Sabina. His monocle indicated that her emotional state was approaching anger. *'Ha-ha silly girl. So young, idealistic, and easy to crush!'* Pierre thought to himself.

Pierre felt shocked when Sabina's emotional state changed from anger to love and compassion. She looked intently at Pierre and spoke:

- You need a hug. You must never have loved or been loved before.

Before he could object to this strange request, Sabina came closer and gave him a friendly hug. As Sabina hugged Pierre, he sensed something he had never felt before. His mind felt at peace, and he wanted to let go of his evil schemes.

"Warning, the girl is breaching your mind. Your secrets will be compromised."

Pierre got back to his senses when his Zetan Monocle flashed in front of his eyes. How long had he been gone? He felt how memories were flashing in front of his eyes, jumbled up in an incoherent order. *'I got to break free.'* Pierre thought and pushed Sabina away. Much to his relief, she allowed him to slip from her grip. As Pierre broke free, he took a deep breath and yelped:

- I did not like that at all. Hugging is not a part of these proceedings. Your time is up, please leave the meeting room now, Sabina and Alex!

Sabina was about to protest, but Pierre signalled his bodyguards to expel them, so they left without a fight. After Sabina and Alex had left, Pierre took a deep breath and asked his bodyguards to wait outside, so he could rest and gather his thoughts about what had happened.

PIERRE WAS CHEWING his fingernails raw and his body was shaking too much to drink his whiskey when he tried to recap the day's events. He was in his Sydney property, which he had bought for the mission to have a secure location where his competitors couldn't spy on him. "Ah, I hate those ugly tapestry on the wall!" Pierre shouted to himself and realised that his mind was in disarray. Sabina posed a serious threat to him and his organisation, and yet he worried about the decorations in his temporary accommodation.

Pierre tried to calm down. Perhaps he had imagined it all. The only thing that had happened was that Sabina had believed that a hug would change his opinion about her proposal to charity funding. After all, she was young and beautiful, so seduction would seem like an effective method to sway elderly men. Then again, why would she bring her doofus husband, if that was her goal?

Pierre calmed down. Sabina had tried to seduce him. The thought that she would use a hug to extract information from his mind was preposterous. Feeling a bit better, Pierre took the whiskey glass to his mouth and enjoyed a sip of its strong smoky flavour.

"Warning, excessive stock market loss detected."

The warning brought Pierre back to an alert and terrified state, when he saw the news that someone was increasing the price of the shares he was shorting. On Monday, he would have to close his shorts as soon as possible and if this continued, he would lose billions. While the loss itself was not the biggest issue, it did prove one thing. Sabina had read his mind, and she was coming after him.

'I BETTER GET VLADIMIR to eliminate that girl at once. We can worry about finding the primordial Zeto Crystal later.' Pierre thought and tried to contact Vladimir via the monocle. There was only silence, as Harapan Conglomerate agents had attacked Vladimir and his group, just moments earlier.

Chapter 20: Do not underestimate the power of the Harapan Conglomerate, 30th March 2040.

Elaine Orchard was feeling tense as she sat in the fortified headquarters of the Harapan Conglomerate in Jakarta, Indonesia. The war with Pierre and Vladimir hadn't started, but yet she hadn't dared to leave the building for two weeks. She needed to secure the support of the other members in the Monocle Conspiracy, but she was afraid of taking the step forward. She couldn't know how they felt about her and Pierre, or which side they would be on.

Elaine knew that Josefina Fiero and Sandra Santiago would be on her side if it came to war. Vladimir had murdered Sandra's father in Nepal back in 2020, and there was no way that they would support Pierre and Vladimir's doings. Apart from them, what about the Mossad leader Szymon Yehuda and CIA's director James Winter? It would be extremely difficult for the Harapan Conglomerate to win a shadow war against the World Bank, the Mossad, and the CIA, even with the help of Josefina and her organisation, Avanço Verde-Ouro Corporation.

"Sabina Hines has left the meeting with Pierre Beaumont at the World Economic Forum. Miss Hines seemed upset."

Elaine looked at the news feed that her Zetan Monocle provided from the hacked CCTV cameras at the Convention Centre. If Sabina Hines and Pierre had come into a conflict, it was likely that Pierre would make a move and send Vladimir to attack her. Elaine needed to stop this from happening. She picked up an encrypted phone and called Budi Sepulyat.

Elaine:

- Budi, it is time. You need to attack Vladimir and his men today. They are going to make a move on Sabina and try to steal the Zeto Crystal.

Budi:

- Understood. Have you secured the support from the other factions yet? Who are we up against except for the World Bank?

Elaine hesitated. She didn't want to lie, but it wouldn't boost the morale to tell Budi that he was up against overwhelming odds:

- Josefina Fiero and her company will help us.

- Do not underestimate the power of the Harapan Conglomerate. We will prevail.

Budi:

- Kami akan menang. Hidup Indonesia dan Konglomerat Harapan. (We shall prevail. Long live Indonesia and the Harapan Conglomerate)

Elaine:

- Good. I have faith in you, my son. Now make me proud.

After hanging up the phone, Elaine felt worried. She had sent her adopted son on a hazardous mission to kill the most dangerous man on the planet. Yet, it was the only way to stop Vladimir's evil scheme to use nerve-pain-amplifiers to terrorise humankind. Uncertain if he would listen, Elaine went down on her knees to send some prayers for Budi's safeguard.

BUDI SEPULYAT WAS SHIVERING from cold as he was hiding in the ventilation shaft in the World Tower, while watching Vladimir Kravchenko.

Vladimir and his crew were presiding in the penthouse level of the building, which was the highest residential building in Sydney. The cold from the heat-reducing suit was necessary to avoid detection from infrared cameras, but it caused severe hypothermia. Budi hoped he would be able to stay focused before his body reached a state of shock, at which point the suit would turn-off to save his life.

Once he was in position, he took aim for Vladimir and waited for his men to move in place. His shot would be the starting point for the battle, and it was crucial that he felled Vladimir with his shot, otherwise anything could happen.

VLADIMIR KRAVCHENKO was drinking Russian vodka to deal with the boredom. He couldn't understand why they had spent weeks in Sydney without moving in on Sabina and steal the bloody crystal. They had concluded that she was unarmed and harmless, and yet Pierre wanted to give Martin Orchard the time to figure out the Zeto Crystal's location.

"Ura!" Vladimir exclaimed as he raised his glass of vodka. Vladimir was knocked back when something hit him in the face. Time stopped, and he saw the bullet that was centimetres from his eyes, frozen in time. '*So, this is how I'll die,*' Vladimir thought and smiled. Time resumed and Vladimir fell to the ground. While still injured, he looked up and glanced at the room. Muzzle flashes were everywhere, and his fellow mercenaries fell in droves to their invisible enemy. '*This must the Harapan Conglomerate's doing, but I will not fall here.*' Vladimir concluded and tried to make his way to the rooftop, while still in pain. He got hit several times, but his body armour took the brunt of his internal damage and he could pinpoint the direction of the invisible opponent that blocked his path to the stairs. It pleased Vladimir when he saw blood streaming out from the thin air, as his enemy went down. Vladimir didn't have the time to study the scene. He made his way to the rooftop and tried to get his monocle to blow up the explosives he had hidden in the penthouse for scenarios like this.

"System crash. Command not available" the monocle showed him. "Damn it to hell!" Vladimir muttered as he pulled up his controller to blow up the penthouse. As he got the controller up, he heard how his pursuers were coming after him up the stairs. 'I rather live to fight another day.' Vladimir thought. He dropped the controller and ran to the hang glider he had parked on the rooftop and jumped off the building.

Budi and Rexi reached the rooftop the exact moment that Vladimir jumped off the building. They shot after him, but were unable to hit him with a killing shot.

Budi picked up the phone and called Elaine:

- We carried out the attack, but Vladimir managed to escape.

There was moment of silence, as Elaine checked on Vladimir's system connectivity via her own monocle. He had disconnected from the network, which was both good and bad. Good, as he wasn't nearly as dangerous without the help of his Zetan Combat mode, but it was also bad as they couldn't trace his location.

Elaine:

- How many dead and wounded?

Budi:

- Three on our side. We killed all of Vladimir's soldiers. We also found out that they rigged the whole level with explosives.

Elaine:

- Get out of there and set off the explosives. We need to cover up the evidence of this battle.

Budi:

- Ratu Elaine, but what about the innocents that will die from the explosion and the debris? They do not deserve this.

Elaine:

- We cannot worry about the few, just carry out my order!

Budi:

- Understood, my queen.

After saying this, Budi gathered his men and set the explosives to blow up the penthouse level. After that, they used their invisibility suits to escape the scene and the approaching sirens of police patrols.

Chapter 21: Pierre requests backup from the Mossad, 1st of April 2040

Pierre was hiding inside his Point Piper mansion. His mind was full of fear. He had lost his private army of elite mercenaries in the fight at World Towers. The forensic specialists had found 40 bodies at the scene, of which 8 were from the NSW police force who had perished when the building exploded. The number of injured was in the hundreds. This was real war.

Pierre had defied the odds by attending the races the previous day to give Martin Orchard an ultimatum. The show had to go on, and under Pierre's order, the media had not covered the massacre at World Towers on the news. For now, the fact-checkers would label anyone reporting about the recent attack as a deluded conspiracy theorist. Eventually, the truth would come out. Before it did, Pierre needed to cover up his ties to the dead mercenaries.

During the Sunday morning, Pierre had caved in to his fears and asked Prime Minister Danielle Anders for protection. Danielle had been happy to comply, and Pierre's residence resembled a fortress rather than a home. Despite being protected by large groups of police officers and army troops, Pierre still wasn't feeling safe. It was humiliating to hunker down like this, under Danielle's "protection". It also made him fearful of the Australian PM as their latest interaction had been less than cordial.

Pierre looked up when an Australian soldier approached him and spoke:

- Hi mate, you've got some visitors.

'Address me as Master Beaumont, you lowly brute!' Pierre thought to himself, but refrained from scolding the soldier and replied:

- I see. Did they identify themselves?

Aussie Soldier:

- They are on this screen here. Their leader introduced himself as Szymon Yehuda.

Pierre:

- I know this man. Please let their leader in. Tell the others to wait outside.

Aussie Soldier:

- Understood. Consider it done.

The Australian soldier left and Szymon Yehuda entered the room. Pierre sneered at him:

- Why did you bring only four men to help me? Do you know what we are up against?

Szymon:

- Tsk, tsk, tsk. Less is more. Assigning only four men to this mission attracts way less attention. Besides, what good are numbers if your men are getting drunk and get slaughtered like pigs?

Pierre:

- Point taken.
- So, do we have an agreement?

Szymon:

- Yes, we will locate Sabina Hines and Martin Al-Sham, kill them both, and steal the primordial Zeto Crystal for ourselves. Once we have secured the primordial Zeto Crystal, we will enact our glorious plan of expelling the infidels from the Holy Land. After that, we'll aid you in your crusade against the Harapan Conglomerate and bring House Beaumont to fame.

Pierre sighed. It was far from ideal that Szymon Yehuda would get temporary control of the primordial Zeto Crystal. But what else could he do? He was at war with the Harapan Conglomerate, Vladimir was nowhere to be found, and Elaine's manoeuvres had Pierre pinned down in this mansion. If Elaine Orchard, Martin Orchard, and Sabina Hines were to join forces, that would be the end of him. Pierre said:

- Yes, we have an agreement.

Szymon:

- Good. Our Sydney branch associates can track Martin, as he has our hidden nano-technology tracking device implanted. We will keep him under surveillance and intercept him when he meets with Sabina.

Pierre:

- Good. Any news on Harapan Conglomerate's activity?

Szymon smirked and replied:

- As I said, we will help you with those inferior South East Asians once the primordial Zeto Crystal is under our control.

- I am leaving you now. We will be in touch if anything changes.

Having said this, Szymon mock-bowed to Pierre and left the room.
Pierre sighed. If he could only get hold of Vladimir. Or in case if Vladimir was dead, find out the truth, so he would know how to proceed.

Chapter 22: We must help Martin Orchard, 3rd April 2040

Budi Sepulyat was spying on Martin Orchard using a nanotechnology drone. Martin was standing close to Barangaroo Wharf. Budi got a sense that something was up when he saw a group of Mossad operatives led by Szymon Yehuda sitting at a nearby coffee shop. Considering that Martin had killed Szymon's brother, betrayed the Mossad, and had given Sabina Hines access to the Zeto Crystal at the Solomon Temple, a confrontation was imminent.

What happened next surprised Budi. Martin Orchard took off his Zetan Monocle and put it in the inner pocket of his suit jacket. Why would he make such a stupid move? Budi knew that the Zetan Monocle gave the user superhuman combat capabilities. Unless Martin wanted to die, it was idiotic to take off the monocle when a fight was imminent.

Budi switched to the screen of the security camera of another drone, and he saw how Martin was approaching Sabina Hines. As he got closer to her, the Mossad agents moved in the direction of them with their guns. Budi turned to Rexi and spoke:

- We got to help Martin Orchard, as instructed by Queen Elaine. The Mossad is coming for him and Sabina Hines.

Rexi:

- Yeah, but they are out in the open. There are tonnes of people out and about today. Do we want a war with the Mossad in front of a massive crowd?

Budi:

- It's unavoidable. We cannot allow the primordial Zeto Crystal to fall into the wrong hands.

Rexi:

- Understood, Budi.

After saying this, Budi and Rexi got out of the van they had been in. They activated their invisibility suits and rushed towards Martin's location, where the ruckus had started.

'*That must be the Zeto Crystal*,' Budi thought, when he saw Sabina Hines take a luminous gem out of her pocket and attack Szymon Yehuda with it.

What happened next occurred in very quick succession. Sabina backflipped into the harbour and with the primordial Zeto Crystal still in her hand. The Mossad agents started shooting after her under the water. Martin Orchard jumped forward, inserted his monocle, pulled out his pistol, and fired off four quick shots which killed the four Mossad agents. Martin got up and exclaimed "Fuck you, Szymon," and offloaded his remaining bullets into Szymon's face, ensuring that he died permanently and would never be able to be revived again.

"Let's go. We need to sedate him and get him out of here."

Budi said and walked behind Martin undetected, while still wearing his invisibility suit. Rexi followed suit, and in a matter of seconds, they had attacked Martin from behind and injected him with a sleeping serum. They had sedated Martin to unconsciousness with their potent sleeping drug, to bring him back to safety. After that, they took out an invisibility blanket, wrapped it around Martin, and hurried back to their van for an immediate escape.

"GIVE HIM ANOTHER SHOT of the Tranquilizer, Budi"

Budi injected Martin with another shot of the high-grade tranquillizer. They needed to keep Martin unconscious, to perform some surgery on him. In order to leave the country undetected, they needed to find and remove the nerve-pain-amplifier chip that Vladimir had implanted.

"I have detected the whereabouts of the microchip, be steady with the scalpel." Rexi urged.

Budi was about to make an incision, when the sudden sound of gunfire distracted him. One of their men, hurried into the warehouse where they based their Sydney underground operations.

- Budi, we are under attack by the Mossad! They are bringing a large
  cohort of soldiers!

Budi:

- Understood. I'll join you in the fight after we are done with this.

Having said this, Budi turned to Rexi and spoke:

- I hope you can remove the microchip on your own. We will need
  to leave sooner than we planned.

Having said this, Budi ran to put on his invisibility suit. Once the suit was operational, he picked up an assault rifle to start the hunting.

Budi got out from a backdoor and he saw a few Mossad agents shooting towards his men. He resisted the temptation to shot them. Instead, he ran in a large semi-circle to reach the Mossad agents' vehicles. Budi twisted the neck of the driver of the large van, and he put a rock on the accelerator to make it go straight ahead. After that, he went ahead to the roof of the building. As the van crashed into a concrete pillar, he used the crowd's confusion to break the neck of two Mossad agents. The destruction of their vehicle caused other Mossad agents to run towards to the van to check what had happened. Budi used this opportunity to throw a hand grenade towards the van to take them out.

The sound of several more cars approaching caught Budi's attention. He had never anticipated that the Mossad had such numbers in Sydney, and retreating was the only option. He ran back to the warehouse, where Rexi had successfully removed the tracking chip from Martin's body.

Budi:

- Let's go.

Rexi:

- How? We are surrounded by enemies.

Budi:

- Put on an invisibility suit and wrap Martin in an invisibility blanket. We'll carry him to safety. I'll rig explosives to the rest of our gear; we cannot let our enemies steal our technology.

Rexi:

- What about the rest of our group?

Budi:

- They knew the risk. Let's go.

Rexi did as Budi instructed. He put on the invisibility suit and wrapped Martin in the invisibility blanket. After that, they carried Martin out of the building, while doing their best to stay out of the crossfire.

After carrying Martin a few hundred metres, Budi pulled up his phone and ordered a self-driving cab. It wasn't the best plan as it would implicate them, but he couldn't carry Martin to the airport. Besides, with a bit of luck, they would be out of the country soon.

A WHILE LATER, THEY arrived at Bankstown airport where the Harapan Conglomerate had hidden a Gulfstream private jet. They got on the plane and prepared to take off. They didn't contact air traffic control as they didn't want to bring attention to themselves. Instead, they dragged Martin onto the plane and set a course straight to the east to leave Australian territory.

Budi:

- Make sure to fly straight to the east until we are outside Australian territory. Fly at a very low altitude, it's the only way to avoid radar detection.

Rexi:

- That would wake up every suburb between here and the coast.

Budi:

- Yes, but it's night, and if we travel without our lights on, the low altitude will stop Australia's radar from finding us. Or would you rather take your chances with the Australian Airforce?

Rexi:

- Understood.

Rexi did as Budi commanded, and although their low flight path woke up half of the city, it stopped the air force radar from detecting them. Once they had reached international waters, they continued their low altitude flight to Indonesian territory. It was a bumpy ride, but it was better than being detected by the Australian Airforce.

Chapter 23: "Must I do everything myself?" 4th April 2040

P ierre Beaumont felt a sense of both worry and relief as he entered the Royal Prince Alfred Hospital in Sydney. He was worried about his recent financial losses. Sabina Hines had, through pumping the stocks he was shorting, caused him a loss of $7billion. While this was only a fraction of his total wealth, he worried what would happen if she kept targeting his investments. He needed to eliminate her as soon as possible, but first, he needed to find out about her whereabouts.

On the flip side, the Mossad's attack on the Harapan Conglomerate outpost had killed or disabled all known enemy agents in Sydney. There were reports about a low-flying private jet that had escaped Australian airspace. This aeroplane would have belonged to his enemies, as one had to be desperate to try such manoeuvre. It was just as good. While it was annoying that Elaine's closest men, Budi Sepulyat and Rexi Lembong had escaped Australia, Pierre was free to move again, albeit surrounded by bodyguards.

Pierre entered the room where the doctors had attached Vladimir to a respirator. His Russian partner was weak but conscious, and Pierre felt less worried about his partner than he had been the last time someone beat Vladimir. 'At least, he won't need nine months in a respirator and alien technology to bring him back to life this time.' Pierre thought.

Upon seeing Vladimir, Pierre felt a burst of irritation. Pierre had reviewed the CCTV cameras from the night of the attack. He had noticed that Vladimir and his group of mercenaries had been intoxicated and taken by surprise. How could they be so careless when a lethal confrontation was imminent?

Pierre reprimanded Vladimir:

- Wake up you big bear. How could you lose all our mercenaries? Why did you get drunk and let those Indonesians take you by surprise?

Vladimir:

- Drunkenness was not why they beat us. Those shifty bastards have developed personal cloaking devices. They butchered us before we even saw them.

Pierre reflected over Vladimir's statement. If the Harapan Conglomerate had developed cloaking devices, they would be difficult to defeat in shadow warfare. But what could he do? Should he opt to research countermeasures to their cloaking devices, or was it better to act fast, and have his agents detonate a nuclear device in Jakarta to destroy the Harapan Conglomerate Headquarters? Pierre turned to Vladimir and spoke:

- What about your Zetan Monocle? Surely it could help you detect them even if they wore cloaking devices.

Vladimir:

- They hit my monocle with the first shot and disabled it. It has been malfunctioning ever since, urging me to find a replicated Zeto Crystal to repair it. I can't even take the damn thing off.

Pierre:

- Well, you should find a replicated Zeto Crystal as soon as possible then.

Vladimir:

- How? I have eight bullet wounds in my legs and the malfunctioning monocle is jumbling up my mind. I won't be going anywhere.

Hearing this, Pierre had one of his hissy fits and exclaimed:

- Must I do everything myself!?

Vladimir kept calm and replied:

- So, it would seem.

Pierre calmed down and apologised:

- I am sorry, Vladimir. I will stage an expedition to get you a replicated Zeto crystal so we can get you back on your feet. There are many of them scattered around the world. It's us against the world now, and I need you by my side.

Vladimir nodded but didn't say anything.
'Jesus Ortega's men have caught Sabina Hines in Mexico.'
As Pierre saw this notification, he knew that he needed to act. He needed to gather a group and travel to Mexico at once. If Jesus Ortega came into possession of the primordial Zeto Crystal, he needed to hand the primordial Crystal to Pierre instead of giving it to Josefina or Sandra. If Josefina were to acquire the primordial Crystal, the situation would get even more complicated!
Pierre:

- I need to go. Jesus Ortega has captured Sabina Hines and I need to convince him to give me the primordial Zeto Crystal!

After saying this, Pierre gathered his Mossad agents and hurried to the airport where he chartered an Orbit Flight to go to Mexico.

Chapter 24: We need to help Sabina Hines. 4th April 2040.

Jared and Eileen were drinking coffee at a small private Mexico City airport, waiting for a flight to leave the country. They had struggled with their mission and had not gotten anywhere. They had failed to blend in, and thus they hadn't been able to find evidence that linked World Bank operatives in Mexico with the drug lord Jesus Ortega.

Jared had convinced Eileen to come with him to Australia. While Columnist Party agents had infiltrated all levels of the Australian government, the same applied to Mexico. By going to Australia, they were at least less likely to get caught in the crossfire between rival gangs, or actual warfare if the Mexican Civil War were to take place.

Jared felt tense when El Gaucho, the right-hand-man of Jesus Ortega, and a group of armed men approached them. He sighed in relief as the Narcos walked past him.

Eileen noticed Jared's tension and spoke:

- What's going on Jared? You look like you saw a ghost.

Jared:

- I thought we were in danger. That man was El Gaucho. He is Jesus Ortega's right-hand-man and one of the most dangerous men in Mexico.

Eileen looked at the group and she noticed that they were all carrying weapons. She whispered to Jared:

- How can they be carrying weapons? What happened to airport security?

Jared:

- I guess airport security officers are not paid enough to argue with the men of the most ruthless drug lord in Mexican history. Our flight is boarding soon. This is not our war anymore.

Eileen shook her head and got up:

- I got to find out what they are up to and warn Ana Moreno. The coup might be taking place today.

Having said that, Eileen walked up to a window and she watched as the men approached a private jet on the tarmac.
Eileen:

- They are kidnapping someone.

Jared:

- Please Eileen. We have done everything we can. This is not our fight anymore.

Eileen:

- Yes, it is. They are kidnapping Australian citizens. They are kidnapping Sabina Hines and her husband Alexander O'Neill.

Jared Pond ran up to the window and stared in disbelief. Why had the famous environmentalist Sabina Hines come to Mexico when a war was about to break out? It made no sense. As the Mexican militiamen were holding Sabina and Alex at gunpoint, it was not a cordial reception. Yet, her folly of coming here was not his problem, and he had little desire to die for it.
Jared:

- They are probably taken as hostages to solicit a ransom. Stupid influencers, what were they thinking?

Eileen:

- We got to help them.

Jared:

- There is nothing we can do for them.

Eileen:

- We can't, but Ana Moreno can. We cannot let Sabina die. Her environmentalist zeal is exactly what the world needs for a better future. We cannot let Pierre and his type crush the forces of good.

Jared sighed:

- What do you suggest we do?

Eileen:

- We must follow the kidnappers to their hideout. Once we know where they are hiding, we can ask Ana Moreno and the Mexican army to help us.

Jared:

- I doubt they would care about an Australian environmentalist when the country is descending into civil war.

Eileen:

- Correct. But she will care about stopping El Gaucho. We must follow the militia and find out where they are hiding. After that we call Ana and give her the coordinates. It's the only way to save Sabina.

"Last call to Sydney for Mr Pond and Miss Lu"

Jared grabbed Eileen and tried to get her to their flight on time. She stood firm and replied:

- No. I am not leaving Sabina Hines to her fate. I am staying. If you leave, this is goodbye.

Jared sighed but he also felt how his love for Eileen had rekindled to how it was when they first met. This was the Eileen he had fallen in love with two decades earlier. She was the brave idealist who risked her own life to uphold her ideals and make the world a better place.

Jared nodded and replied:

- Okay. You win. Let's get a vehicle and follow them to their hideout.

After saying this, Jared and Eileen hurried to the airport drop off area and bought a run-down car with cash to continue their pursuit.

JARED AND EILEEN WERE hiding in the bushes at a hill overlooking the complex where the militia had taken Sabina. The mosquitos, insects, and humidity made their lives uncomfortable, but Jared had bigger problems. They had missed their flight to Sydney, and they were hiding in enemy territory.

As they studied the complex below them, they realised that they couldn't get in to save Sabina and Alex. There were too many guards to even consider that idea.

Eileen picked up her phone and turned to Jared:

- We'll need to give Ana Moreno, Sabina's location. It's the only way to save Sabina.

Jared:

- No. The Mexicans might consider Sabina Hines to be collateral damage and attack the building with artillery and fighter jets.

Eileen:

- I trust Ana. She wouldn't do that.

Jared:

- Very well. Follow your instinct.

Eileen nodded and she picked up her phone to call Ana Moreno:

- Ana, I need your help. An Australian environmentalist, Sabina Hines, is being held hostage in the Valle de la Cantimplora.

Ana:

- I am sorry, but I cannot help you. The capital is a powder keg, and I must focus on the situation here.

Eileen:

- I understand your situation, but she is being held by El Gaucho. I can send you a photo to prove it.

There was a brief silence before Ana replied:

- I understand. This changes things. Can you repeat their location?

Eileen:

- Yes. Valle de la Cantimplora in el Parque Nacional Cumbres del Ajusco.

Ana:

- Understood, thank you, Eileen.

Eileen:

- Ana, please bring her out alive. Sabina is crucial to building a better future.

Ana:

- We'll do our best.

After speaking to Ana, Eileen turned to Jared and spoke:

- We did it. Ana promised to send help. Everything will be okay.

After hanging up the phone, Eileen sent the photos she had taken of El Gaucho kidnapping Sabina. Jared smiled at Eileen, but he didn't say anything. Deep down he feared that involving the Mexican army would condemn Sabina and Alex to their deaths.

Chapter 25: "She made the dogs kill Jesus."
4th April 2040

J ared and Eileen were overlooking Jesus Ortega's militia complex from a nearby hill when artillery shells and rockets started raining down on the complex. In the ensuing chaos, a car sped through the gate, but due to the smoke and fire, Jared couldn't make out who was in the car before it disappeared from his view. Eileen felt upset and exclaimed:

- No! Ana, what are you doing?

Jared:

- I am sorry, but I anticipated she would do something like this.

Eileen sobbed:

- But she promised...

Jared:

- She must protect her country. To her, stopping el Gaucho is more important than saving Sabina. What would you have done?

Eileen sighed and replied:

- I don't know. I was never a good president, was I?

Jared:

- Let's reflect on that later. We need to get Ana to stop bombarding the complex if Sabina is to have any chance of getting out of there alive.

Eileen:

- Yes, I'll call her now.

Eileen picked up her phone and called Ana. As Ana answered the phone, Eileen heard gunfire in Ana's background:

- Eileen, I cannot speak to you now, the fighting has taken to the streets of Mexico City, and Jesus' men are in the outskirts of the city.

Eileen:

- Can you please stop the bombing at Valle de la Cantimplora?

Ana:

- We already have, we are focusing on other, more important targets. *Beep, Beep, Beep*

Eileen stared at her phone as the connection broke. In the distance, she heard artillery bombardments in the city, 20 kilometres to the north. Eileen turned to Jared and spoke:

- We need to move. We need to go down there and find out if Sabina is still alive.

Jared:

- I'd rather not. We carry no weapons and there must be surviving militiamen down there.

Eileen:

- Aren't you the greatest agent Australia has ever seen? Isn't danger your second name? Are you going to let the girl save the day? I am going in!

Jared sighed. Being 'the greatest agent Australia had ever seen' had given him an interesting life of booze and sexy women. But now, it was a dangerous title that forced him to do something he rather wouldn't do. Jared got up, started walking to the complex, and said:

- I'll lead the way. Let's save Sabina and Alex from El Gaucho!

Eileen smiled. Jared was still a doofus, but a lovely man, and she felt more alive than she had felt for many years.

SANDRA SANTIAGO WAS feeling terrified as she was hiding from Sabina and Alex in a shed in the jungle. Sandra had taken off her Zetan monocle to visit Sabina in Jesus Ortega's basement. She had taken it off to hide her real associations and to gain Sabina's trust. Sandra had planned to convince Sabina to give her the primordial Zeto Crystal. Once she had the crystal, she would get herself to safety in Brazil while the Mexican Civil War played out.

Sandra's plan had come to naught. Somehow Sabina had gained control over Jesus' attack dogs and directed them to become silent and deadly assassins, who used coordinated attacks to kill everyone in the complex, including Jesus Ortega. To make matters worse, the government had started bombing the complex. Sandra had barely escaped with her life when she drove Sabina and Alex away from the complex. Sandra called Josefina Fiero via her Bluetooth headset.

Sandra:

- She made the dogs kill Jesus.

Josefina:

- What are you talking about? Is something wrong?

Sandra stammered:

- The Aussie girl, Sabina Hines. She controlled the minds of Jesus' attack dogs to kill everyone in the Valle de la Cantimplora complex. I had to pretend to be her friend to get out of there alive.

Josefina:

- Good. You are doing things according to plan. Is there anything I can do for you?

Sandra:

- She is forcing me to drive her to the Sun Pyramid. Send people to help me.

Sandra didn't pay attention to Josefina's answer as she heard terrible screams outside. She grabbed a pistol from the shed and ran outside to inspect the noise. What she saw shocked her. Blood covered Sabina's face, and Sandra's monocle lay on the ground with Sabina's bloodied eyeball attached to it. Sabina placed her primordial Zeto Crystal on her right eye socket, and it instantly grew back and she was unhurt. Sandra was shocked at this and stuttered:

- What's happening? You are not a normal girl. You lost an eyeball, and yet you have two healthy eyes? You look unhurt!

Sabina:

- I am sent by the True Maker to save the future of humankind. There is still time to save yourself, Sandra. Tell us why you have this monocle and repent your sins.

Sandra:

- No. I don't believe you. I saw what you did to Jesus' men. Even if you kill me, the others will deal with you.

Alex, who stood close to Sabina, shouted:

- This is your last chance, Sandra. Help us and save yourself.

Sandra lost her nerve and shot Sabina in the kneecap. Before Sandra had the time to shoot again, a misfired artillery shell impacted with her body and knocked the others to the ground. After a while, Sabina and Alex got up, and Sabina used the primordial Zeto Crystal to heal them. Once they had healed their wounds, they got into Sandra's car to resume their drive to the Sun Pyramid.

"WHAT HAPPENED HERE?" Eileen exclaimed as they entered the complex and saw a militiaman with a ripped throat.

Jared studied the wound. It looked like an animal had slit his throat with its teeth, but the man was armed with an assault rifle, so how had this happened? Jared picked up the gun and spoke:

- We are not here to investigate. We need to find Sabina and Alex.

They hurried to a building on the other side of the courtyard. It was the only building that hadn't been partially destroyed by rockets and artillery fire. Jared had a foreboding feeling when he saw blood flowing down from the stairs. Eileen saw it and exclaimed:

- Devils must possess this place. I am not going up there.

Jared:

- Devils or militiamen, in any case, you are not safe standing here out in the open.

Eileen nodded and she followed Jared upstairs.

They entered the room, which was full of dead militiamen and dead attack dogs.

Jared saw the dead bodies of El Gaucho and Jesus Ortega in the room. He heard the dying breaths of another man:

- Jared Pond. I can't believe you are here.

Jared looked at the man. Despite the man's mauled face, Jared recognized him. The man was Matthew "The Jackaroo" Warner, a RAKI agent specialised in overseas assassinations.
Jared:

- Matthew. What are you doing here?

Matthew coughed up some blood and wheezed:

- Danielle Anders sent me to kill you, and to help Jesus Ortega kill Ana Moreno. Please forgive me, Jared.

'I thought people asked God for forgiveness when they were dying.' Jared thought but he held back his sarcasm and replied:

- I forgive you, Matthew.
- Do you have any evidence against Danielle Anders?

Matthew:

- Yes, it's on a secret server. You'll find the link on my phone. My code is 4645.

Having said this, Matthew closed his eyes, and his breathing became weaker. Jared exclaimed:

- Eileen. Please help me, he is bleeding out.

Eileen shook her head and replied:

- No. We must broadcast the evidence of Jesus Ortega's death to the world. It's the only way to stop the Civil War.

Jared realised that Eileen was right. "Rest in peace, Matthew." He mumbled, got up and started filming Eileen Lu for a live stream where she announced that Jesus Ortega and El Gaucho had perished.

After filming the stream Jared collapsed to the floor and started crying. Eileen kneeled next to him, stroke his hair, and spoke:

- I am sorry for your loss. Who was he?

Jared:

- His name was Matthew "the Jackaroo" Warner. I was his mentor at RAKI. He was the closest I ever had to a son.

Eileen:

- And he came to Mexico to kill you?

Jared:

- Yes, my life story feels like a bloody Shakespeare play now.

Eileen:

- At least the Jared I know would find it funny that Mexico's deadliest man, and Australia's deadliest man, had nicknames that meant the same thing.

Jared smiled a sad smile and replied:

- Yes, it's like I have always said. It's not the sharks you need to worry about, it's the cows.

Eileen smiled as she comforted Jared. With a bit of luck, they had saved the Mexican population from senseless war and killing. If that was the case their trip to Mexico was worth it. Once Jared had calmed down, they stole a car and drove to a peaceful village far away from the capital to wait for the war to end.

Chapter 26: The face-off in the Sun Pyramid. 4th April 2040.

Pierre Beaumont was feeling exhausted as he sat in a World Bank office in the Northern outskirts of Mexico City. This was the longest day ever, as Pierre had travelled past the dateline, and thus, Tuesday 4th April 2040 had already lasted 30 hours for him.

Pierre looked at a tactical map outlining the fronts in the Mexican Civil War, which had started today. 60 kilometres to the south, in the southern suburbs of Mexico City, chaos had broken out. Pierre hoped that he could trust Jesus' promise to not attack the northern parts of the city.

If everything went according to plan, the battle between Jesus Ortega and President Ana Moreno would be a one-sided affair. While the Mexican army was a lot stronger than Jesus's rebels, the troops that protected the capital wasn't. This was because World Bank operatives had bribed Mexican generals to withdraw their troops from the southern part of the capital. Pierre followed the advancement of Jesus' rebels on a tactical screen. They had advanced and were only 20 kilometres away from the presidential palace. Would Ana stay in the palace or would she try to escape? Pierre had prepared for both scenarios.

Pierre picked up his phone and called Jesus Ortega. It bugged him that Jesus hadn't answered his call one hour earlier. If Jesus became the president, he would need to prioritize Pierre's phone calls.

'Incoming priority information. Transferring data.' Pierre's Zetan Monocle displayed. After that, it showed a live feed where Eileen Lu declared that Jesus Ortega and his right-hand-man, El Gaucho, were dead. Pierre panicked. If Jesus was dead, the revolution against President Ana Moreno was leaderless and likely to fail. What would then happen to La Prensa de La Muerte Dam project?

Pierre's mind got back to a more urgent issue when his monocle intercepted a phone call between Sandra Santiago and Josefina Fiero. Apparently, Sabina Hines was behind Jesus' death, and she was heading to the Sun Pyramid. Pierre didn't know what she was after at the Sun Pyramid, but he did know one thing. He needed to kill her and steal the primordial Zeto Crystal. He could not allow her to interfere with his plans any longer.

Pierre walked to another room and spoke to the Mossad agents that had accompanied him from Sydney. Pierre:

- We have located the woman who caused the deaths of Ben and Szymon Yehuda. Bring torture devices, it is time to get vengeance and find out who she works with.

The agents nodded, and a few minutes later, they were in a helicopter for the short flight to the Sun Pyramid, where Sabina and Alex were heading.

AS PIERRE'S HELICOPTER landed on the temple grounds of Sun Pyramid, a few security guards approached him. One of them shouted:

- No puede aterrizar su helicóptero aquí. Este es un monumento protegido por la UNESCO. (You can't land your helicopter here. This is a UNESCO protected monument)

"Fuck this shit!" Pierre muttered to himself, initiated combat mode on his Zetan Monocle, and shot the security guards in quick succession. After that, he shouted to his men:

- Anyone else got something to say?

The agents looked away, and a short while later they entered the inner sanctum of the temple area. The needless killing of the security guards had filled Pierre with adrenaline. Under normal circumstances, he would have used his money and power to bribe the guards. However, since he was in a country during a civil war, it was more satisfying to eliminate the problems.

Pierre directed his monocle to search for Sabina, and it showed him three potential heat signatures underground in a tunnel. 'I see, she is going to the Royal Tomb.' Pierre reflected and he directed his men to follow him. As they reached the Royal Tomb, Pierre shot the guide that waited outside the tomb and he entered the room accompanied by the Mossad agents.

Pierre stared in awe at the room and the primordial Zeto Crystal, which Sabina held in her hand. The primordial Crystal was glowing of a beautiful blue shining light, and the room looked so bright and luminous, different from Pierre's last visit to the complex. Pierre spoke to Sabina:

- What a beautiful sight. I love what you did to the room, Sabina.

Sabina gave Pierre an angry look and replied:

- So, we meet again. Why did you murder our guide?

Pierre sneered sarcastically:

- Well, we can't leave any witnesses behind for our little ordeal, can we? Like a speck of dust, his puny little life on this planet is now over. But it doesn't matter. By tomorrow this country will have descended into civil war and chaos. Hahaha!

Sabina:

- So, are you starting a war just because I am here?

Pierre:

- Don't be ridiculous. This war was long in the making. It is a consequence of the Mexican government's refusal to pay back what they owe us.

Sabina:

- But they won't be able to pay you back if you destroy them.

Pierre laughed hysterically:

- Ha-ha! Money is an artificial human construct. There is something even more important than money itself, and that is the power that money symbolizes. Besides, I have an unsurpassed ability to generate wealth from any forms of disaster.

Sabina:

- So, why are you coming after me?

Pierre continued with his sarcasm:

- You started this conflict between us, dear Sabina. You should never have pumped the shares that I was shorting and won against me. But an even more important reason for me to be here is the primordial Zeto Crystal, which you have stolen from us.

One of the Mossad agents walked up to Pierre and spoke:

- Mr Beaumont, we need to wrap this up, the frontline in the civil war is moving towards us.

Pierre nodded, turned to Sabina, and spoke:

- Mrs Hines. While I enjoyed speaking to you, we need to wrap things up. Give me the primordial Zeto Crystal or I'll kill you and your husband Alex.

Sabina:

- I am not giving you the primordial Zeto Crystal. You'll try to kill us no matter what I do.

Pierre smirked and replied:

- I won't just try to kill you. I will succeed as I always do. Neither of you will leave the Sun Pyramid alive!

Sabina shook her head and defied Pierre's taunt:

- No, you won't! Your evil reign ends tonight, Pierre Beaumont. This is your last chance to repent and save yourself.

'Hmmm... She seems so assured of herself, is she bluffing, or have I walked into a trap?' Pierre thought to himself. One thing was certain. He couldn't back down now. He had to double down on his threats. Pierre aimed and shot Alex in the kneecap. Pierre laughed as Alex collapsed in pain:

- Oh, that looks like a nasty wound. Tsk, tsk, tsk, lucky I got some medicine.

Having said this, Pierre took out a vial of poisonous acid and threw it into Alex's wound. As the acid dissolved into Alex's kneecap, it started to boil, and Alex screamed in excruciating pain from the toxic acid burn. Pierre taunted:

- I don't have all day, but I can spare some time to make Alex's death a painful one.

The same Mossad agent as before spoke again:

- Why don't we just shoot her, Monsieur? If the pyramid gets hit in the bombardment, this tunnel will collapse, and we are done for. We must hurry!

Pierre smirked at the agent and replied:

- Silence, Melchior. There is a method to the madness. You'll see.

"Very well. I accept your demands. Give me the antidote to Alex's poison."
Having exclaimed this, Sabina threw the primordial Zeto Crystal to Pierre, who instinctively caught it.
As Pierre caught the primordial Zeto Crystal with his hand, Sabina chanted some alien language prayers: *"Simba.... Zetani..... Humanis!"* This activated the Crystal's auto defence mechanism and set Pierre ablaze with a white luminous flame. As the Mossad agents stared at Pierre's ghastly death, Sabina bent

down to pick up the primordial Zeto Crystal and Pierre's pistol. A short fire-fight broke out, and afterwards, everyone in the room except for Sabina were dead.

Sabina collapsed to the floor and uttered a short prayer to her deity, The True Maker. After that, she used the Zeto Crystal to revive and cure Alex. This self-blasting procedure that killed Pierre and the healing powers that cured Alex had drained the energy of the primordial Crystal, so Alex and Sabina left the Pyramid and hurried to Pierre's helicopter. They highjacked the helicopter and forced the pilot to take them to the airport where their private jet was parked. After that, they quickly left Mexico. Sabina's mission was still ahead of her, but she couldn't stay in Mexico any longer as she had more important things to do.

Chapter 27: Deaths and a new beginning, 10th April 2040.

Jared Pond and Eileen Lu were waiting at Mexico City airport. The civil war was over, as Pierre Beaumont's sponsored coup led by Jesus Ortega had died when their leader was mauled by his own attack dogs. Jared had found the evidence that Danielle Anders had sent Matthew Warner to kill him and President Ana Moreno. He had published the evidence online, and the news had viralled like wildfire. This had forced Danielle to resign, with a pending investigation on her coup against President Moreno. The ordered assassination of Ana Moreno was a huge scandal, as it was an unprecedented act of war between Australia and Mexico. Jared smiled. Even though Danielle Anders seemed to have more lives than a black cat, she would not find a way out of this mess. Particularly not since Pierre Beaumont and the media would no longer support her.

Eileen Lu was drinking Bloody Mary and Jared a glass of Long Island tea when a few guards from the Mexican presidential office approached them. One of them spoke:

- Senor Pond and Senora Lu. Please come with us, President Ana Moreno would like to speak with you before your departure.

Jared:

- Why isn't she coming herself?

Guard:

- Please Senor Pond. Which President in her right mind would show herself in the open six days after a failed coup, which ended thousands of lives? There are plenty of Jesus Ortega supporters out there, looking for revenge.

Jared:

- Very well. We are coming with you.

Jared and Eileen followed the guards to the VIP section of the airport, which was behind a bulletproof one-way-mirror. Eileen flinched when she saw what was on the other side of the mirror. President Ana Moreno was accompanied by several agents from the infamous Ministry for State Security from the Columnist Party of China, seemingly in agreement with each other. Ana smiled at Eileen and spoke:

- Miss Lu. Thank you for saving me and my country from Jesus Ortega's coup.

Eileen:

- And this is how you are rewarding me? By handing me right into the hands of the people who seek to murder me.

Ana:

- It is not as simple as that. Li Jing Xi from the ministry will explain it to you.

Li Jing Xi spoke to Eileen:

- First of all, let me be forthcoming with you. You murdered my biological father, Chairman Jing Xi. Shortly afterwards, you took the presidency which ended in a massive catastrophe.

Eileen tensed up. Was this the end of her? Couldn't fate let one good deed go unpunished?

Li Jing Xi gave Eileen an unexpected smile and spoke:

- Don't worry, Eileen. Murdering the tyrant Jing Xi was in fact a good deed. My mother was one of the many unwilling concubines he forced himself upon during his reign of villainy.

Eileen:

- I assume you did not come to thank me for murdering him, so why are you here?

Li Jing:

- Your situation is a conundrum to the Columnist Party. On the one hand, we want to eliminate you for deposing us from power and murdering Jing Xi back in 2021. On the other, I am glad that my cruel father died by the hand of an ex-journalist.

Eileen:

- I did not do any of this. I was Jing's prisoner, and he was about to rape me when his secretary turned on him to save me.

Li Jing:

- Debatable but irrelevant. However, there has been plenty of water under the bridge and we are thankful that you stopped Pierre Beaumont from taking control over Mexico.

Jared:

- So, why don't you let her go? Cross Eileen off your hit list if she promises to not involve herself in Chinese politics anymore.

Li Jing:

- Well, it's not that easy. The two of you are wanted in Dubai for the murder of Peng Yingxing, Eileen's deceased husband.

Jared:

- We didn't kill him. He had a heart attack.

Li Jing:

- Also, debatable. Regardless, the Emir sees things differently. You've embarrassed him, Eileen. He can't accept women disobeying his orders, he wanted you to stay married to Peng for political reasons. Even if he can't get you extradited to Dubai for a mock trial, he will send assassins to kill you.

Jared:

- So, no matter what, we'll have assassins coming after us.

Ana:

- Not necessarily. I've discussed the issue with Li Jing Xi and together we found a solution. We'll give you both new identities and Mexican passports while China will provide you with wealth that will last you a lifetime. Jared Pond and Eileen Lu both died as heroes, stopping the drug lord Jesus Ortega from overthrowing the Mexican government. From now on, Mr Jakob & Mrs Ellie Bond can live a happy life as retirees in the Caribbean.

Eileen:

- But our faces are known worldwide, it will never work.

Li Jing:

- The Ministry for State Security has some of the best plastic surgeons in the world. The Australian Prime Minister Danielle Anders used to be a man working for us, we have excellent cosmetic surgeries which will make you look completely different.

Jared:

- I knew that Daniel and Danielle were the same person.

Li Jing smirked:

- Yes, but less than 50 % of the Australian voters did. Some even thought he had been kidnapped by aliens and woke up as a female.

- Anyways, this is the best we can offer you. If you refuse, we won't do anything to protect you from the Emir's men.

Jared had a look at Eileen. Could he imagine retiring and spending his remaining days on a Caribbean paradise island with her? Yes, he could.
Jared:

- I would be happy to accept this offer and retire together with the one true love of my life.

Eileen:

- I am sick of fighting and I am sick of people around me dying. I would also be happier with a new identity as Jared's wife.

Ana:

- Excellent. We will take you to a medical facility to do the cosmetic procedure. Your new life should be due in 6-8 weeks.

After saying this, Eileen and Jared followed Li Jing Xi to a discreet plastic surgery clinic.

JAKOB BOND WAS NOW having a quiet night at their secluded mansion in the Caribbean together with his wife Ellie Bond. He had been going on a spin on the jet ski to get the adrenaline up, but apart from that, there was no danger in his life anymore. Jakob looked at his reflection in the mirror and sighed.

"Look what they did to my face. No-one would believe that I once was Jared Pond, the greatest agent Australia had ever seen.

Ellie smiled, kissed Jakob, and replied:

- That was the point of the surgery, my love.

Jakob teased:

- At least they let me keep one good part...

Ellie:

- Indeed, that part is still the best Australian agent that no one else sees. *wink*

For a moment, Jakob felt melancholic that his past excitement of espionage, booze and great looking women was now over. But then he remembered that he retired with his one true love, and that he could always relive his prime years with her every night.

Chapter 28: Epilogue.

Below is the ending for all the main characters throughout the **The Banker Trilogy**.

Sabina Hines went on a holiday in Hawaii to recuperate. The holiday didn't last for long as Elaine and Martin kidnapped Alex to force Sabina on a daring mission. Sabina travelled with Martin to the Sunken Pyramid of Kiribati where she opened a portal to another dimension to confront her nemesis, the Xeno empress Rangda Kaliankan. After killing Rangda, Sabina activated the kill switch on all the monocles. This killed everyone in the Monocle Conspiracy except for **Martin Orchard** who vowed to get revenge. Sabina and her daughter, Keila, lived until Sabina was 112 years old, when they sacrificed themselves through letting their bodies absorb the gamma-ray-burst that was destined to destroy Sydney. To read more about Sabina's adventures, please check out my book **Sabina Saves the Future Trilogy.**

Martin Orchard felt convinced that Rangda Kaliankan was a threat to mankind, so Martin forced Sabina to come on a quest to stop Rangda. After surviving Sabina's attack on the monocle users, Martin swore to avenge Elaine's death and his own disfigurement. He did this through trying to destroy Sabina's reputation and convincing Sabina that Rangda possessed her daughter. After getting his revenge, Martin retired and stopped committing atrocities. Martin died from a morphine overdose after contracting terminal brain cancer in his late 60's. To read more about Martin's lifetime of villainy and adventures, please check out my book **The Fall of Martin Orchard.**

Jared Pond & Eileen Lu lived cushy lives as retirees under their new identities. Eileen involved herself in charity projects but stayed away from politics. Jared got his adrenaline from jet skiing, Scuba diving, and hiking. They led active lives and they died together in their late 80's from a flu that wasn't hyped.

Vladimir Kravchenko had barely recovered from his wounds when authorities arrested him for causing the Hei Bai virus outbreak in 2021. Mass arrests followed and the World Bank was dismantled for the organization's crimes against humanity. Vladimir died before facing court as Sabina activated the kill-switch on his Zetan Monocle.

Elaine Orchard rekindled the flame with her ex-husband Martin and died when Sabina activated her kill-switch. The Harapan Conglomerate passed on to her adopted children Budi and Rexi, and they focused on utilitarian projects to heal the damage that the company had caused.

Josefina Fiero was busy destroying evidence and contesting an extradition when the kill-switch put her out of her misery. Her company was split up into smaller parts after her death.

James Winter was facing court for his involvement in the 2028 assassination of Eva Moreno, when the monocle kill-switch ended his days.

Damien Vanderbilt served two terms as the US president after Eva Moreno's assassination. When the truth came out, Damien was pardoned by his successor, but that didn't help against the angry mob that lynched him.

Ana Moreno resigned as the Mexican president six months after the civil war had ended. She sought refuge in China under a new identity and she started writing left-wing-literature until her death many years later.

Danielle Anders hung herself while awaiting trial for her treasonous act to send an assassin to murder a foreign head of state. People speculated for a long time whether Danielle committed suicide or if she was murdered.

Frank van Stein died while using Vladimir's technology to resurrect **Delphine Beaumont.** Delphine continued her father's legacy of villainy and murder. However, without his technology and wealth she didn't last long, and she ended her days admitted to a psychiatric institution.

Don't miss out!

Visit the website below and you can sign up to receive emails whenever Martin Lundqvist publishes a new book. There's no charge and no obligation.

https://books2read.com/r/B-A-QIOG-RVMLB

BOOKS 2 READ

Connecting independent readers to independent writers.

Also by Martin Lundqvist

Divine Space Gods
Divine Space Gods: Abraham's Follies
Divine Space Gods II: Revolution for Dummies
Divine Space Gods III: Rangda's Shenanigans

La Trilogica Divina Zetan
La Divina Disimulación

Sabina räddar framtiden
Sabinas jakt på den heliga graalen

Sabina Saves the Future
Sabina's Pursuit of The Holy Grail
Sabina's Quest to Open the Portal in the Sun Pyramid
Sabina's Expedition to Stop the Apocalypse

The Banker Trilogy
The Banker and The Dragon
The Banker and the Eagle: The End of Democracy

The Banker and the Empath

The Divine Zetan Trilogy
The Divine Dissimulation
The Divine Sedition
The Divine Finalisation

Standalone
Matt's Amazing Week
James Locker The Duality of Fate
The Portal in the Pyramid
Money Laundering in the Laundromat
Pyramidportalen
Matts Fantastiska Vecka
Divine Space Gods Trilogy
Sabina Saves the Future: Complete Trilogy
Diez Historias Aleatorias y Muy Cortas
Ten Random and Very Short Stories
10 zufällige Kurzgeschichten Volumen 1
Dieci Storie Casuali e Molto Brevi
Dix Histoires Aléatoires et Très Courtes
Cinco Historias Aleatorias y Muy Cortas
Five Random and Very Short Stories
The Fall of Martin Orchard
Masa Depan Putri Sabina
La Caída de Martin Orchard
El Banquero y el Dragón
A Sedição Divina
Dieci storie casuali e molto brevi. Vol 2
Δέκα Τυχαίες και πολύ Σύντομες Ιστορίες Volume 2
The Coldvir-20 Killer
10 zufällige Kurzgeschichten Volumen 2

Förkylningsmördaren

Watch for more at martinlundqvist.com.

Lightning Source UK Ltd.
Milton Keynes UK
UKHW022041260123
416041UK00005B/137